D0949723

Holding On to Zoe

GEORGE ELLA LYON

Holding
on
to
Zoe

Margaret Ferguson Books
Farrar Straus Giroux ◉ New York

Lyrics to the songs on pages 71 and 110 were written by George Ella Lyon.

The poem on pages 122–23 is "Fire and Ice" by Robert Frost, from *The Poetry of Robert Frost: The Collected Poems, Complete and Unabridged* (Henry Holt, 1979).

Farrar Straus Giroux Books for Young Readers
175 Fifth Avenue, New York 10010

Distributed in Canada by D&M Publishers, Inc.
Printed in the United States of America
Designed by Alex Garkusha
First edition, 2012
10 9 8 7 6 5 4 3 2 1

macteenbooks.com

Library of Congress Cataloging-in-Publication Data
Lyon, George Ella, 1949–
　　Holding on to Zoe / George Ella Lyon. — 1st ed.
　　　　p.　cm.
　　"Margaret Ferguson Books."
　　Summary: After sixteen-year-old Jules loses her boyfriend she experiences complications from the pregnancy that drove him away, and suddenly, some of the people closest to her are behaving as if her baby is not real.
　　ISBN 978-0-374-33264-8 (hardcover)
　　ISBN 978-1-4299-5528-7 (e-book)
　　1. Pregnancy—Fiction.　2. Teenage mothers—Fiction.　3. Mothers and daughters—Fiction.　4. Emotional problems—Fiction.　5. Single-parent families—Fiction.　6. Babies—Fiction.　I. Title.

PZ7.L9954Hol 2012
[Fic]—dc23

2011009832

For Jutta Kausch,
Jacky Thomas & Jimmy Stevens—
healers, teachers, friends

Holding On to Zoe

one

I SWEAR I WON'T WORK IN THAT FACTORY one day longer. It is killing my legs, my ears, my back. Tending the line that puts door handles on minivans, that's what I do: sweeping to make sure nothing's underfoot for workers and taking production numbers from the foreman to the supervisor. The machines count, of course, but they want a human count, too. All day I hear the zing and whump of the machines, feel the vibration that aches my bones. Halfway through the afternoon I tell myself, You're never coming back. You don't have to. Nobody can make you.

Then I get off my shift, walk the long hall to the day care, and as soon as I feel the warm weight of that baby in my arms, I know I'll go back. I've only had this job a few weeks. I'll get used to it. I have to. How would I pay for her diapers otherwise? How would I afford her doctor? How would I pay our rent?

Why am I working in that factory day after day anyway? Why did I leave high school, my best friend Reba, and Mom's little apartment to take this job and move to an apartment at Toyota?

Zoe is the answer. Zoe is the answer to everything.

Of course, I used to think the answer was Damon. Damon of the curly brown hair and the smoky dark eyes, Damon who was so moody and funny, humming and winking at you one minute, gone off inside himself to some dark place the next.

I still think I loved Damon: the way he walked down the hall at Stuart Ellis High like he was about to step out on a stage where fans were waiting, the way he loved music so much he didn't have time for English and history but spent exams drawing guitar fingerings which he turned in instead of answers, the way he wrapped me in his strong arms and sang to me after.

Sex was okay but it didn't give me what I thought it would, didn't bring me any closer to understanding Damon—or even to feeling close to him. That's pretty funny, isn't it? Here this guy is inside your body and still you don't feel you're with him. It was in the singing afterward that I felt close. Close and held. I would have given a lot for that. I did give.

And after I missed my period, when I told Damon about Zoe, he said he would marry me, just like that. His dad was a truck driver, never around, and my dad had skipped out years ago. Damon said he'd be damned if he'd let his kid grow up that way.

I couldn't believe this. I thought he'd offer to go with me to the doctor, maybe contribute to the cost of an abortion. So when he said he wanted to marry me and have the baby, I envisioned a whole new life. We would be a family—Mama, Daddy, baby! I laughed and cried. We were huddled on the wall of the skateboard park near the school. I'd been so sad and scared, I couldn't believe what I was hearing. I wasn't alone. Damon put his strong arms around me—I remember his navy blue sweatshirt smelled like cigarettes and fabric softener—and I rested against him, a little bird safe in the nest. Till the nest flew away. Damon told his mom that night and she yanked him out of school the next day and sent him away. Just like that.

He didn't even tell me in person. He called me from the Greyhound bus station the next afternoon.

"Hey, Jules—"

"Are you sick? Why weren't you in school?"

"I'm sorry," he said. "I told my mom and she threw a fit. She's sending me to Tennessee to work construction for my Uncle Rick."

"She's what? What about school?"

"She said I'm about to flunk out anyway, which is true.

But the thing is, Jules, working construction is really bad for my hands."

"Your hands?" I couldn't believe what I was hearing.

"Yeah. Guys get fingers smashed and tendons torn all the time. It could ruin my guitar playing."

"Damon," I heard my voice getting higher. I was pacing the small box of our kitchen and about to hyperventilate. "What about our *baby*, our *family* you were so sure about yesterday?"

"Grow up, Jules. Like Mom says, we can't have a baby. We're kids."

"But we *are* having a baby, Damon. You can leave town but I'm still pregnant."

"I know. And whose fault is that? Anyway, when I get paid I'll send you some money to help get rid of it."

"*Rid of it?*"

"You know what I mean."

"I do, but I can't believe you. Yesterday—"

"Yesterday I was a kid, pretending. Now I'm a man with a job that I've got to get out of fast. Got to make my way to Music City. At least at Uncle Rick's I'll be in Tennessee, that much closer . . ."

My throat was hurting like I wanted to cry and my heart was pounding like I wanted to scream, but I just said, "Is there a phone where I can call you?"

"I don't know where I'm staying yet," Damon said.

"Maybe with Uncle Rick, maybe with one of his friends. But I'll let you know. You'll see. I'll make it up to you. When I'm playing at the Bluebird Café in Nashville—"

Talk about fantasy, I thought. "But you won't be here," I said. "I need you *here*."

"Sorry, Jules. They're calling my bus."

"I'm sixteen and pregnant," I said. "And the daddy of my baby is skipping town."

"Sounds like a country song," Damon said.

I hung up.

I stood in Mom's kitchen, my finger threaded in the black loops of the phone cord. I felt as alone as if Damon had never happened. Cast out of the circle we'd made, that small hot space where I had tried to feel at home.

I took a deep breath. Think of a *good* thing, Jules, I told myself. There's got to be one. Oh, yeah. Your mother wasn't here when he called. That's it. Things could be worse. Lana Livingston McCauley could be standing in this room.

And she will be home from work before long, I realized. I'd better get hold of my life while it *is* my life.

The first thing I do is look across the breakfast bar, through the living room and out the grimy window. We're on the second floor, but I know that beyond the parking lot, diagonally across Willow Street, is a laundromat.

Well, that'll be handy, I think. I can wash the baby

clothes right across the street. Mom always says it takes too much time to wait on the machines in this building. There are only four and usually one is out of order. Plus they're in a dank dingy room. Gross.

I have to have this baby, Damon or no Damon. I can't be alone anymore. Of course I'm not feeling sick or cosmically sleepy yet. That comes later. I don't feel weird at all, unless you count being sure of something as weird, which I guess it kind of is for me. Before Zoe, I was always looking around to see how I was supposed to be, picking up signals from my parents first and later, after Dad left and Mom was too busy, looking to other kids for clues.

Sometimes I'd try to talk to Mom like my best friend, Reba, talks to her mother—try to sound casual, connected. Like one day when she got home late, I said, "Hey, Mom, there's a new Chinese place on Weber. Reba's mom says it's great. I could go pick some up and you wouldn't have to cook."

She ran her hand through her short hair, put out her lower lip, and blew air up till it lifted her bangs. Exasperation. Then she said, "Jules, may I remind you that we are *not* the Karims? Your father is not a lawyer—he was a private pilot, for heaven sakes. And at this point I don't know what he is except gone. I don't have the luxury of staying home like Sara Karim, and we do *not* have money to throw around."

"I know, Mom. Sorry."

"It's not just our expenses, I've still got school loans to pay off."

"I know, I know." After Dad left, Mom had to go back to school. Her part-time office work wasn't enough, so she went to college and became a social worker at the same place she used to file and type.

When Damon and I first got together, I even tried to be like *him*, saying books bored me, ignoring homework, trying to buy into his dream. He'd make it big in music one day and we'd travel and see the world. I liked imagining this but I couldn't *be* Damon. I wanted stuff to think about, too. I wanted my own dream. That's how I am. Also, when it came down to it, I had to do well in school. For Mom.

Anyway, my days of trying to be like somebody else or blend in are over. Now that I'm pregnant, forget it. Every day that passes, I will be less blended in.

And it turns out that I have a voice inside me that knows her mind. Maybe she was always there but I never listened before. Maybe it was that one speck of boy juice that nested itself in the egg and changed me. I don't know. I just know when I quit looking to other people for directions, I found my own map.

It's late January. My baby won't come till the end of summer at the earliest, so I can finish my junior year. I'll keep my part-time job at Baskin-Robbins until I start to show, and then when the baby comes, I'll have to find a better job and finish school somehow.

Think, Jules, I tell myself. What do people with kids do? Kids with kids?

No, what can *I* do? Me, Juliet McCauley, always called Jules. Me, somebody's mother.

two

FOR A FEW WEEKS I DON'T DO ANYTHING but go to school, scoop Rocky Road, do homework, and grow Zoe. I don't tell Mom or Reba. I am sickish in the morning, but not throwing-up sick, though smelling the ice cream—especially piña colada—makes me gag. And my thinking has changed. When Mr. Turner, my AP history teacher, talks about the Challenger explosion (it's the first anniversary), about how brave the astronauts were, especially Christa McAuliffe, the first teacher in space, I think, but she was a *mother*. She didn't just leave the earth. She left her *children*. How could she do that?

Then, on the day after Presidents' Day, I am talking to Reba outside precalculus when bam! just like that, I throw up onto one of my clogs.

"Jules!" Reba exclaims. "Gross!" Then, "Are you okay?"

"Yeah," I say. "Do you have any Kleenex?"

She digs in her backpack, then hands some over and

says, "Hold on. I'll get some paper towels from the bathroom."

Reba disappears around the corner while I dab at my shoe and the floor with a wad of pink tissue.

Waves of heat and yuck flap through me like a flag till I squat and finally sit back, resting my head against the wall. Kids step around me like I'm a trash can set there to catch a roof leak, but when Mrs. Feeback, our teacher, shows up, she sees me. "Jules, what's wrong?" she asks. I look up at her and the concern in her face makes my eyes sting.

"A bug, I guess. I don't feel so good."

"Why don't you go see the nurse? Maybe you should go home."

"Okay," I say, though they won't dismiss you to walk and I know Mom won't take off work to come get me.

As Mrs. Feeback slips into class, Reba reappears. She has dry towels for the floor and a damp one for me to wipe my face. While I press the cool brown paper over my eyes, she does the janitor thing.

"Thanks, Reeb," I say. "Who would take care of me if I didn't have you?"

"Don't breathe on me, Jules. I don't want your germs."

I laugh.

"I'm serious," she says. "I hate throwing up."

"I don't think you can catch this," I tell her, "but if you could, mopping up would probably do it."

"Yeah, right," she says. "Tell Mrs. Feeback I've gone to wash my hands."

"Without a pass?" I ask. The bell for first period is ringing.

"I've got the puke pass," Reba says, holding up the hand with the towels.

I give Mrs. Feeback the message, then walk to the office, trying to think of something to tell the nurse. Turns out I don't need to worry. She isn't there. This one woman, Mrs. Ratliff, is the nurse for two high schools. I don't know about the other school but we've got 2,500 kids here. You'd think that would be enough for one nurse. When Mrs. Ratliff's not here, she deputizes office workers or volunteer moms to hand out pills, give shots to stop diabetic comas, call 911, etc.

"Mrs. Feeback sent me," I tell the secretary. "I just threw up."

"Do you need to go home?" she asks, punching the phone button to transfer a call.

"I can't," I tell her. "My mom's at work."

"Well, go lie down in the nurse's room," she says. "If you keep throwing up, you'll have to go."

"All right," I say. "Are there any crackers in there?"

"Should be. On a shelf by the desk." Her attention turns back to the phone. Then she calls, "You're not diabetic, are you?"

"No."

"Fever?"

"I don't think so."

Curled up on the cot in Mrs. Ratliff's office, I reckon with the fact that I am going to have to tell Mom soon. Like maybe tonight. No, no, my scared self says. You can't. She'll—

She'll what? I ask myself.

She'll be so mad—

Well?

She'll yell at me and then—

Then?

She'll be so disappointed. She's got too much to deal with already. She'll say I've ruined everything. Like when I broke my ankle, only worse.

She's always disappointed in you.

Yeah, but this is major. I can't—

Sure you can. You've got to, I tell myself. It's not like she's going to hit you.

I wish she would.

Don't be stupid. Mom never, ever hits you.

Maybe she should. Then I could defend myself. I could be mad at her.

If you want to be mad, be mad at Damon.

Right. Fat lot of good that would do. It's not like I can call him up and yell at him.

With that thought, followed by a few wimpy tears, I fall asleep.

three

I WAKE UP IN TIME for second period and make it through the rest of the day. When I see Reba in the bus line next to mine, I ask if she can hang out for a while.

"Sure, if you're feeling okay," she says. "I'll walk over as soon as I get home."

"Great."

It just seems to me if I tell Reba first I'll get some practice at saying "I'm pregnant" out loud and some practice at dealing with what comes after. I am so scared. How could you do this to your mom? I think. Your mom who's worked so hard all alone to raise you right?

But I didn't *do* this, I say. I didn't decide to get pregnant, not really. Okay, maybe I decided once not to NOT get pregnant. I didn't even exactly decide to have sex, though there was a moment when I might not have. And Damon, for all his speed in leaving the scene of an accident, did not pressure me.

I just thought I had to do it. You want this boy to like you, right? And he's so solid, so sure of himself. He knows what he wants: you. Besides, maybe if he touches you, you'll be real.

For a guy, Damon was very responsible. He always took time to dig for the foil packet in his jeans pocket on the floor of the car, to tear it open and try to apply the rubber, which kept popping off like a hat that's too small, making us laugh, even as he trembled. Finally he would get the damned thing on. I'd already put in the foam. We thought we were safe. I know Mom will say, "Jules, how many times have I told you: No sex is safe"? So hey, Mom, you're right.

When Reba shows up at the apartment, we head for the refrigerator.

"Coke?" I ask.

"Sure."

I bend down to the bottom shelf where the cans are. "Hungry?" I ask.

"Always," she answers.

Setting the cans down, I reach around to open the cabinet with the Triscuits. Reba is standing on the living-room side of the breakfast bar, staring at me. I avoid her eyes.

"What's up, Jules?" she says, sliding the scünci off her ponytail so her blond hair hangs in stripes down her black sweater. She puts the scünci over her wrist. "You're acting weird."

"I'm thinking about Damon," I say, pouring Triscuits in a bowl.

"Earth to Jules: I can eat them out of the box."

"Oh, yeah," I say. "But Damon—"

"Did you hear from him?"

"No."

"So . . . ?"

"So I'm pregnant."

Reba takes a cracker out of her open mouth and brings her hand down to the bar. Her blue eyes widen.

"Oh my God," she says, looking at me like my hair is on fire. "Are you sure?"

I nod.

"Those tests can be wrong," she says.

"Not if your breasts feel like very sore headlights and you're throwing up." I've read about this in *What to Expect When You're Expecting*, which I checked out of the library with some other pregnancy books.

She keeps staring like I am some kind of disaster area. "Stop looking at me like that!" I say.

"Sorry!" Reba says, and eats the Triscuit. "But this is a shock. You didn't even tell me you guys were fooling around."

I didn't and I don't really know why. Reba and I have never kept secrets from each other. Not before this. I try to make a joke. "Oh, no, we weren't fooling around. It was having lockers on the same hall that did it."

"You're not very pregnant are you?" Reba asks. "You've got time to get rid of it?"

Damon's words. I don't say anything. Now it's my turn to stare.

"I can help if you need money," she offers. "Maybe you don't even have to tell your mom. You know how she is—"

I take a sip of Coke, counting on the sweet bubbles to settle my stomach.

"I have to tell her. It's my baby. I can't get rid of it."

"Jules! Are you nuts? It's not a baby! It's a ball of cells that will wreck your life if you don't stop it!"

"No, look!" I unzip the side pocket of my backpack and pull out *The Nine-Month Miracle*. "See?" I flip to the eight-weeks photo, the gray traveler with the tiny body curled under its bulby head. "It's not just cells. It's a baby!"

"This is serious," Reba says, like I don't know. "We're kids! What about camp counseling this summer? We were going to do that together! What about senior year?"

"I'll get a GED, I guess," I tell her. "Or finish by correspondence. I haven't thought that far."

"Sounds to me like you're not thinking at all!" Reba says, her cheeks getting red. "You can't have a baby, Jules. You've lost your mind. This isn't some dollar movie—"

Now I am mad, too. "Don't you think I know that?"

She reaches across the bar and takes hold of my shoulders. "It's your life, Jules," she says, shaking me just a little. "Your only life."

"But not just mine," I blaze back. "I'm sick of mine."

"Whoa," she says, letting go. "Okay, girl. Listen to me. Pregnancy has put you in some kind of hormone crisis. I want you to take your Coke and crackers and go lie down. I'm going home. You go to sleep, and after a good nap, I want the real Jules to call me."

"Some friend you are," I say. "I knew my mom would act like this, but I thought you—"

"The real Jules," she cuts in.

And as I head back to my room, she puts away the crackers and then lets herself out the door.

four

IT'S NOT THAT REBA DOESN'T MAKE SENSE, I think, stretching out on the tiger-striped spread we bought at the old hippie emporium. I would have said the same thing before Christmas, before this new life started. From the outside that's how things look. Reba sees a roadblock that has to be removed. I see a road. What will Mom see? I reach over to my bedside table, raise up enough to take a sip of Coke, then as soon as my head hits the pillow, I am dreaming.

I am walking around the block at our old house, in the neighborhood where we lived before Dad skipped town. I am coming to the Fraleys' house with its mimosa tree in front that was always full of tent worms. Afraid one of those squirmy things might fall on me, I'm about to cross to the side of the street where Larry, the paperboy, lived when Mrs. Fraley calls out to me from the porch.

"Skinny-bones," she says. "Can you jump double Dutch?"

"Of course I can," I tell her.

"Show me," she commands, standing up from the glider

with the end of a jump rope in each hand. The other ends are tied to the tree and Mrs. Fraley starts turning.

This would never work in real life, I know—not double Dutch, especially not with porch steps—but in the dream it does, and I start jumping right on the sidewalk up to her house. Mrs. Fraley calls out the rhyme:

Skinny-bones, Skinny-bones, turn around.
Skinny-bones, Skinny-bones, touch the ground.
Skinny-bones heart, Skinny-bones mind.
Skinny-bones carry what you find.

With that, the caterpillar tents infesting the tree light up like lanterns, and scare me so bad I jump out of the turning ropes, catching one foot so that I stumble but don't fall. I can hear Mrs. Fraley laugh as I run down the street and turn the corner.

There is more to the dream but that's all I remember. I do not feel good when I wake to hear Mom coming through the front door.

"Jules?" she calls.

"I'm in here," I call back, reaching over to turn on the light. Mom comes down the hall and into my room.

"You sick?" she asks.

"Yeah," I say. "Well, I felt sort of bad at school this morning, so I thought I'd take a nap when I got home."

"It's not your period, is it? I can't stand girls who make a big deal over something that's perfectly natural."

I interrupt this intro to her familiar lecture. "No, Mom. It has nothing to do with that." Though, of course, in a way it does.

"Probably a bug, then," Mom says dismissively. "Both of Elly's kids are sick." Elly's another social worker in her office. "And Deb says half the kids at her daughter's day care are out, too."

I nod. "You don't have a fever?" she asks, standing there in her winter-smelling coat. She's not the type to put her hand on your forehead.

"No."

"Good. Could you eat tacos?"

My stomach folds over. "I don't think so."

"Scrambled eggs then," she declares.

That sounds slightly less awful, so I say, "Sure, Mom."

"I think I'll take a shower first," she says. "Crazy people at work today."

Mom works for the state, in the office where people come to apply for disability. She says most social workers complain of the paperwork, but it's the stories that wear her out. It wasn't so bad at first, but the longer she's worked there and the more she's seen "people whose problems have problems," as she says, problems there's no way she can solve, the more she's gotten allergic to stories.

"Tough clients?" I ask.

She nods. "Today there was a lady who thinks she leaves her body every night and has an astral affair with the man next door. They're both married and she swears she's never looked at him twice, but now she feels guilty every time she sees him across the driveway because she thinks it must be happening to him, too, and this makes her so nervous that she makes mistakes in her job as a beautician—like stripping hair she was supposed to highlight—and therefore we, her fellow citizens, should pay for her upkeep while she recovers from this handicap."

"Will we?"

"I don't *think* so," Mom says.

As she's telling this, I'm thinking how desperate grownups are but then I wonder, if this woman got pregnant, would she only be pregnant at night? Would she have an astral baby?

I muse on this as I get up and set the table. And I forget to call Reba.

I don't tell Mom that night. I just can't. Twice at dinner I start sentences that could lead to saying it, but I change direction before I get there.

The first time, I start with Damon. "Mom, I told you about Damon moving away?"

She nods, buttering her toast.

"It's just—well, I really miss him, Mom. And I don't even have a number where I can call him."

"Didn't you tell me he dropped out of school?"

"That's right."

She shrugs. "Trust me, Jules. You don't want to get involved with somebody who has no future."

Involved? Oh, Mom, I'm about as involved as anyone can get. And as for the future, it's right here. I eat a forkful of eggs, a corner of toast. I try again.

"When I was sick this morning—"

"Maybe it was those Pop-Tarts," Mom cuts in. "I know that stuff is bad for you. Cardboard and sugar. I was just rushed. I'll make muffins in the morning."

"No, Mom. It's not that."

"Well, what then?"

She looks at me sharply, daring me to tell her something she doesn't want to hear. Does she know? Could she?

"The thing is, I threw up on my shoe."

"That's appetizing, Jules. Thanks for sharing."

"I just want to know how to clean it."

"I'd say a little hand soap and water on a paper towel. Then some shoe polish, if we had some, which we don't. Maybe a dab of vegetable oil so the leather doesn't dry out."

"Okay."

"Jules—"

Oh God, I think. Now she's going to say it.

"Maybe this boy will see the light and get hold of himself and come back to school. Then you might think about him. But for now you need to concentrate on the possibilities in front of you."

Oh, I am, Mom. If you just knew . . .

"Your school work . . . who you are becoming . . ."

I let her wind down, then say, "Mom, if you're finished, I'll just do these dishes and get on with my homework."

"Okay," she says, rubbing the bridge of her nose.

"Headache?" I ask.

She nods, then shakes her head, so that her golden star earrings are swaying. "You wouldn't believe the messes people get in, their pathetic lives . . ."

"I can imagine," I say.

"I doubt it!" she says, and laughs. Mom has a little heart-shaped face and hazel eyes that still have light in them, headache or not. It's only Tuesday night of a long work-week, and already she's too tired to hear what I have to say. And too young to be a grandmother.

five

THE NEXT MORNING I GET SICK ON THE BUS. I have an aisle seat and I've brought some wet paper towels in a Ziploc bag just in case, so I clean up the worst of it. I can't do anything about the pandemonium it sets off, though.

"Barf alert!"

"Get back!"

"Look out, guys—she's gonna hurl!"

"Oh, man. They'll have to let me out the back door. I'm not stepping over that."

"What is it?" Mrs. Hayes, the driver, barks over the mic to the left of the steering wheel.

"Vom at zero hours!" someone calls out.

"Who's sick?" Mrs. H. asks wearily.

"It's me," I holler back. "Jules McCauley. Can I get off and walk back home?"

"Against school policy," Mrs. Hayes replies. "Once you're on this bus, only the school office can dismiss you."

"Abandon hope all ye who enter here," Jacob Basiri puts in.

Once inside school I head not for the office but for the bathroom, where I get rid of the plastic bag and wash my face and hands. I look at myself in the mirror. My skin is the negative white of no-fat milk and would look better with lime green spiked hair than mine, which is dark brown, shoulder length. My eyes look vague and wary at the same time. Wanted-poster material. So now what, Jules? Now what do you do?

Go AWOL and skip school? No, Mom would get an automated call and then I'd have to explain that.

Go to precalculus? And risk throwing up in front of Mrs. Feeback again? I don't think so.

Call your mom to come get you? No.

Nurse? She's probably at the other school. Besides, I'm not sick.

Counselor? Hmm.

I've never gone to Ms. Adams except once for a scheduling problem, but I know she helped Reba when Mr. Pike took a dislike to her in English class and kept grading her down. Reba marched in with her test alongside Dan Simpson's, which had the same answers but got a better grade. Ms. Adams cleared up the grade and moved Reba to another class in a heartbeat. Suddenly, in the feeble, flickering light of the math hall bathroom, Ms. Adams seems like the answer to a prayer. She fixes things. She helped Reba with Mr. Pike; maybe she could help me with Mom. This is hormones talking, hormones that just got here, that never lived with Mom or went to school before.

I leave the bathroom and head for her office without even considering that I have no appointment. Luck seems to be with me because Ms. Adams calls me in right away. Her small office is bright with travel posters and pictures of a baby, a toddler, and a little blond boy who I decide are all one kid: hers. I hadn't noticed these pictures when I came before, and now they seem like good news.

"Have a seat, Julie," she says. "What's going on?"

"He looks like you," is what pops out of my mouth.

"Who?" She follows my gaze to the picture on her desk. "Oh, Richie! That's my sister's son. Isn't he adorable?"

"But he's so blond, like you," I stammer.

She stretches a strand of curly blond hair in front of her face.

"Mine has help!" she says, then laughs. "How can I help *you*?"

"I threw up on the bus this morning," I say.

"Yes?"

"And I threw up yesterday in front of Mrs. Feeback's room."

Ms. Adams sits up straighter in her chair, giving a little tug to her blue-green sweater. "Shouldn't you be in the nurse's office?" she asks.

I look at the poster for Madrid behind her. I want to step under the arc of that cathedral door into a great darkness . . .

"Julie?"

"I think I'm pregnant," I tell her.

"Ah ha," she says, maintaining her smile though some of its friendliness leaks away. "That would do it."

I nod.

"Does the father know?"

"Yes," I say. "But he's not—he's not in town." I start to tell her all about Damon, but for some reason I don't.

"How about your mother?" she asks.

"Not yet," I say.

She puts her fingers together in front of her, spider-fashion. "Well, you know, Julie—"

"It's Jules. I'm called Jules."

"Jules. You are not the first girl to walk in here with this problem."

I nod.

"And over the years I've evolved a standard way of dealing with it."

I nod again.

"It is imperative that your parents—"

"My dad's out of the picture," I put in.

"Okay," she says, picking up in her sentence again, "imperative that your mom know immediately."

"No, please!" I say. "Not yet." My heart starts jumping around wildly. "That'll just make it worse. I mean, I'm going to tell her. I'm just not ready. I came to you for help—"

"Slow down, Jules. I know you did. And that was the right decision. You put the information into my hands. And I will hold it for a week. If your mother hasn't confirmed that she knows in that time, I'll have to tell her myself."

I feel sick. Different from the nausea, this bitter juice is fear zapping my stomach. I feel betrayed, even though I know Ms. Adams is right: I have to tell Mom.

"If you can't do it at home," Ms. Adams continues, "I can call her in here."

"Oh no," I say. "She hates taking off work to come to school." At this point tears prick my eyes, which makes me mad. I am pregnant, not pathetic.

"Do you want me to call your mother and say you're ill and she needs to pick you up?"

"No, that's okay. Really. I'm better now. I'll go on to class."

"You're sure?"

"Sure," I say, standing up.

Ms. Adams stands up, too, and holds out her hand. "It'll all work out," she says. "Don't worry."

"Right," I say, shaking her hand. I pretend she's congratulating me on the baby, knowing she has no more clue than I do.

Then I head for humanities class. I've missed precalc, the only class I have with Reba. I'm thinking I'll catch her at lunch, but she doesn't show up. At first I worry, then remember, it's Wednesday, paper staff day. They bring lunch and meet in Mr. Hill's room. I'll have to call her when I get home.

six

BUT I DON'T. Planning how to tell Mom overshadows everything else. I decide I'll do it right before I go to bed so we won't have the whole miserable evening to get through. I'll clean up the kitchen after supper, study for my French test—yeah, right—take a shower, and then when she sits down in her green velour robe to watch the news, I'll say, "Speaking of news . . ."

I'm actually walking through this in my mind as I stand in the kitchen sipping Coke when Mom opens the door at five-thirty.

"I'm pregnant," I say across the breakfast bar. Just like that. Horrified but relieved, too. No more hiding.

The air in our dim apartment shifts. It's like when the band is on the field at halftime marching and playing and suddenly they reverse direction.

Mom does not yell. She doesn't curse or cry. She puts down her purse and takes a deep breath. "Don't be ridiculous!" she says.

"But it's true," I insist. "I've missed two periods—"

"You!" she says, like the word is something disgusting she has to get out of her mouth. "Girls your age have erratic periods. You don't know what you're talking about."

"I threw up on the bus," I say. I sound like a little kid. I hate that.

"Germs, Juliet. Everybody gets them."

"But Mom, my breasts hurt."

"Stop your drama!" she commands. "No child of mine is getting pregnant at sixteen!"

I nod. "I'll start my homework," I say.

"You do that."

I go to my room, shaking with cold and anger or fear or something. As soon as I shut the door I realize my backpack's in the living room. Oh, never mind. It's not like I could focus on anything anyway. My teeth are chattering, so I crawl into bed, hoping sleep will get me out of this trap, at least for a little while.

I sleep for three hours, then wake up to silence and a note from Mom on the counter. "Here's dinner," it says, with an arrow pointing to the box of saltines and can of chicken soup alongside. "I have a class to learn about new software. Love, Mom."

Love? Does she mean that? It's hard to tell. I expected

to be relieved to have told Mom, to have that part over, no matter how mad she was. How could I think me being pregnant would make *her* any different? Sheesh! That was dumb.

The phone rings. I reach across the fruit bowl and a basket of bills to where the receiver hangs on the wall.

"Hello?"

"Jules! Are you okay?" It's Reba.

"More or less," I say.

"You never called me."

"I'm sorry, Reba. I got sick on the bus this morning and went straight to see Ms. Adams. She said I *had* to tell Mom right away . . ."

"So you told her?"

"Yes and no," I say.

"Go on."

"I told her but she didn't believe me."

"She didn't believe you were pregnant?" Reba's voice goes high with amazement.

"That's right."

"Wow! Your mom is *so* not like my mom. What are you going to do?"

"I haven't thought that far," I say. "I went to sleep after she yelled at me and I just woke up."

"My mom would have been hysterical," Reba says.

"I know." I can picture Mrs. Karim's pink cheeks blazing with anger and then her eyes getting blurry with tears as she hugs Reba. I can see her closing the yellow kitchen door with its "Keep out unless you're bleeding" sign so she and Reba can talk in private.

"My mom would have a fit and then make tea and then call the doctor."

"I know." I think a minute. "That's what I need to do. Call Dr. Brennan."

"Won't that make your mother mad since she doesn't believe you?"

"Well, yeah. But you know what? I've got to stop thinking about my mom and start thinking about my baby." This cheers me up somehow. I take a deep breath. My stomach feels unsettled all of a sudden, so I pinch the phone to my ear with my shoulder and open the crackers.

"Jules—" Reba's voice has that about-to-give-advice sound.

"Don't say it."

"I just don't think you're thinking straight," she says.

I hang up.

In all the years I've known Reba, which is since our moms enrolled us in Coop Preschool, I've never hung up on her. No matter how mad we got at each other, we never—

The phone rings again.

"Don't do that," she says, before I even get out Hello. Her voice is thick with tears. "If I have to be an aunt, I'll be an aunt, but talk to me, Jules. Don't act like you've moved to another country."

"That's sort of how I feel."

"Well, consider this a transatlantic call. How will you, a sixteen-year-old kid, take care of a baby?"

"It can't be that hard," I say.

"Jules, you don't even like babies."

"I've never had one," I point out. "This isn't babies. This is *my* baby. It's all I've got."

"Can I say something?"

"Go on."

"I think you've been taken over by aliens. You remember what we read in health—you've got a million hormones flowing through your body and they've sabotaged your mind. They've hijacked the teenage Jules and left this—"

"I'll call the doctor tomorrow after school," I cut in.

"Good."

"Yeah, I know. I need special vitamins. They said that in health, too."

"Aieeee!" she exclaims. "What you need is your old brain back."

I rummage in the drawer under the stove for a soup pan.

"You've taken up drums?" Reba asks.

"No, I'm cooking. Well, heating soup."

Reba sighs. "Okay, Jules. You eat your soup. I'm going to play Nintendo till my brain is loose enough to face precalc. We'll get back to this after you talk to the doctor."

"Sounds good," I say, hanging up. A few minutes later, the soup is bubbling. It smells strange, sharp like canned cat food.

seven

WHEN I CALL DR. BRENNAN'S OFFICE the next afternoon, they say to come on over. He's had a cancellation. Luckily, his office is in walking distance of the apartment.

I *want* this baby, so it makes sense to go to my real doctor. He can send me to a baby doctor. For that matter, he can convince Mom I'm pregnant. She listens to him. She listens to men, actually. Strange, since she's always telling me not to trust them. "I fell for your dad," she says, "and I'm still falling." I muddle over this as I walk the three blocks to the doctor.

As soon as I give the receptionist my name, a nurse appears. "How's Miss Jules?" she asks as we walk back.

"Good," I say.

"And what brings you in today?" she asks, opening the door on a pale green ice-cold examining room.

"I'm—" I lose my nerve for a minute. "I think I'm pregnant."

The nurse's expression doesn't change and I am grateful. "Dr. B. will want to do a pelvic then."

She reaches in one of the examining table drawers and pulls out a paper gown.

"Take everything off below your waist," she instructs, "and put this on with the opening in the front. Dr. B. will be in as soon as he can."

She pulls a curtain as she leaves.

I get out of my jeans and into the big crinkly paper napkin, climb onto the examining table, and stretch out. Pretty soon I am shivering. Then I feel sick to my stomach. I close my eyes.

Dr. Brennan's gentle voice startles me. "What's wrong with our girl?"

I sit up, surprised. The nurse didn't tell him? "I'm—at least I think I'm—pregnant," I say.

"Well," Dr. B. says, looking at me. Even when Mom was here to tell him what was wrong with me, Dr. Brennan always wanted to hear my version. It must be the same now. His blue eyes stay gentle and he runs his left hand over his disappearing hair. "You've missed a period?" he asks.

"Two," I say.

"Any other symptoms?"

"A couple of mornings I threw up," I tell him.

"You've done a home test?"

I shake my head. I let Reba think I had. "I can just tell," I say.

"And you are . . . sexually active?"

"I have been," I say.

"Well, then. While I get the nurse to set up for a pelvic, I want you to collect a urine sample. You remember how to do that?"

I nod.

"Down the hall to your right, third door. All the supplies are there."

I put my coat on over my paper gown and leave the room. Ten minutes later I am on the table on my back and Dr. B. has me put my feet in these metal contraptions that look like eyelash curlers. They force your legs into a crouching position so you're all opened up for the exam. Not good!

Then, sitting on a stool at the end of the table, with the nurse standing behind him, Dr. B. turns on a bright light. Sort of like being at the dentist, I think, only at the wrong end. And the light is warm. Before touching me, he holds up a clear plastic tube.

"This is a speculum," he explains. "It holds your vagina open so I can see. It'll be a little cold going in but it shouldn't hurt."

"Okay," I say.

"Just relax."

He slides the speculum in. It doesn't hurt exactly but

my left side feels tight all of a sudden. Before I can say anything, he takes it out, saying, "Hmmm. Now I'm going to use my hand to check your ovaries. This may be a bit uncomfortable. Just take deep breaths."

I feel his fingers go in and reach to the right. He puts pressure there, from inside with his fingers and from outside with his other hand. I breathe. Then he moves his hand to the left and a hot ball of pain explodes where he touches. I scream.

"I'm sorry," Dr. Brennan says. "Easy now. We're done."

I feel his hand leave but a lesser pain is still pulsing and tears pour down my face. My legs start shaking. I'm so glad Mom isn't here.

"Mrs. Davis, could you get her a blanket?" Dr. B. asks the nurse as he straightens my legs, and folds in the stirrups. "You feel better?"

I nod, still trembling. Cold and hot. "What's wrong?"

Mrs. Davis comes back in with the results of the urine test and a white thermal blanket, which she and Dr. B. spread over me. It feels like love.

"I can't be sure yet," he says, careful with each word. "You *are* pregnant, but I think you have an ectopic pregnancy, which means the egg implanted in the fallopian tube rather than your uterus. I'm sending you for an ultrasound to be certain."

"What about the baby?"

"You don't have to worry about the baby. There won't be one."

He tells me this like it's good news.

"No!" I say, tears clogging my throat. "It's my baby! You can't take it away!"

"You've had a shock," Dr. Brennan says. "We'll talk after you get dressed." He is out the door.

The nurse puts her arm around me and helps me get down from the table. I'm still shivering as I pull on my jeans and turtleneck.

When Dr. Brennan comes back, he motions me to have a seat, then sits on the silver rolling stool. "The office is calling to make the ultrasound appointment," he tells me. "Then they'll call your mother to come get you."

"Please don't!" I say. "Don't bother her at work. It's not good. I'll tell her about the appointment."

Dr. Brennan looks at me gently. His brown-rimmed glasses have slid down his nose, showing off his bushy gray eyebrows. "Does your mother know about this?" he asks.

"Yes," I tell him.

"Hmm. I'm surprised, then, that she didn't come with you."

"She doesn't believe me," I blurt out.

"Oh." A pause. He rolls the stool a little closer. "A good reason for me to talk with her." My heart starts racing and I put my hand up to protest, but he says, "Can you go straight home and rest?" I nod. "And when does your mom get home from work?"

"Five-thirty."

"Good. I'll call her just before I leave the office. How's that?"

Terrible, but better than calling her at work.

"Okay," I say. "But you're wrong about the baby."

He takes a deep breath, then puts a hand on my shoulder. "The ultrasound will clear things up," he says.

eight

WALKING HOME I REALIZE HOW IT IS. The baby isn't stuck. She's waiting to make sure she's welcome. The bad energy of Damon walking out and Mom not believing me would give anybody the creeps. So I just have to concentrate all of me on being a home for this baby, being the right place and the right time. Then she can move on to where she needs to be. She feels like a *she*.

"I'm your home," I tell her, as I step over the slush to cross the street at Dearborn. "I'm getting ready for you."

My side pinches as I walk fast, but it's too cold to go slow. Steady, I tell myself. Ahead is Mom coming home and Dr. Brennan calling. I could panic about that. But it wouldn't be good for the baby. They'll just have to learn, Mom and the doctor both. Mom refuses to know a lot, and he doesn't know everything. But you can't ignore a baby.

Mom has just hung up her coat and put on the teakettle when the phone rings. I'm sitting on the couch pretending to read but I feel like I'm in a waiting room. Like at the dentist, only worse. Mom doesn't even know I've been to the doctor. Strike one. She hasn't even sat down. Strike two . . .

"Hello. Yes?"

Pause.

"Dr. Brennan? What—"

Pause.

"She did *what*? I told her—"

Pause.

It's clear Dr. Brennan doesn't know how to talk to my mother. Interrupting her just fuels the fire.

"I *told* her she wasn't having a baby!" Mom gives me a look that would peel paint.

Oh, Baby, I think. Hold on. The storm is about to break. Remember, I believe in you. Whatever happens, you've got me.

"If you're absolutely sure it's necessary," Mom says, hissing those *s*'s.

Pause.

"All right, then. Tomorrow at four. I'll have to leave work early, but—"

I realize I'm holding my breath. I'm sorry, Baby. That's probably not good for you. My breath is yours, too. Thinking this makes me almost happy, which is insane in this situation.

Click.

"Juliet McCauley, I cannot trust you for one minute."

She strides over and stands above me. "Here I am off doing my job, believing you are doing yours, and instead you're going behind my back seeing Dr. Brennan all because of this"—she slashes her right hand out like an umpire calling half-safe—"this *ugly* fantasy that you could have a baby. What is wrong with you?"

I try to speak but she rushes on.

"Isn't life hard enough without you turning it into a soap opera?"

Shreee! The teakettle whistles. "Come in the kitchen," she commands, turning her back. I follow.

Oh, Baby, oh, Baby, I say inside. Rough waters, but I'm your boat.

Mom's anger is too big for the little kitchen. She yanks the cupboard open, snags a mug, rattles the tins on the counter getting her tea bag. Pours. Don't burn yourself, I'm thinking. Be careful. She is. She sets the mug on the table, jerks open a drawer to get a spoon.

"Milk," she says. I get it. "Stop staring and sit down."

I do that, too.

"Because of you, I'll lose time tomorrow and have to make it up."

I nod.

"Because you let some boy, that Damon, *use* you—"

"He didn't use me, Mom. I want this baby. I want her."

"No!" she shouts, jumping up, hitting the table, sloshing

the tea. "We will spend time and money and set people talking about you for nothing. It's a mistake, not a baby. And they'll cut it out."

I'm up now, too, as tall as she is. I get right in her face but she comes at me, and I back up to the stove, where my elbow hits the hot kettle.

"Owww!" I am louder than the kettle was.

"Stop it!" she says, hands on my shoulders, shaking me. "You're not hurt!"

"No," I say, steady, big as her. "I'm pregnant."

I push past her and go to my room.

When she calls me to supper I say I'm not hungry. I can eat the rest of the crackers in my backpack. We don't speak the rest of the night.

The next morning she tells me, "Be ready at 3:45."

"Don't worry. I will."

She gives me a look and is gone.

I get through school without throwing up, and I already have my coat on when Mom gets home. I've been testing it to see how big it is. I put my backpack on in front. The coat wouldn't button over it. Oh well, by the time I'm that big, it'll be warm.

Weirdly, Mom wants to talk on the drive.

"Let me tell you something, Jules," she says, before we're

even to the corner. "When your dad took up with Rachel Meyers and left town—"

What? "Dad left *with* somebody?" I cut in.

She goes on. "He most certainly did and never looked back. And one of the worst parts of it was being pushed into such a clichéd story: dumb woman blind to her husband's affair. Rachel was my friend, you remember."

I shake my head.

"My *best* friend, she lived around the corner from us, next to Larry, the paperboy."

"I don't remember her," I say. "But I kind of remember Larry." A big boy with puffy lips.

"Well, it's an old story, a rerun since the Bible, since Abraham and Sarah . . ."

She talks on but I'm still stunned. Dad was in love with somebody else and they both left? Are they still together? This could be good news. Maybe they have children. Maybe I have a sister! "Where did they go?" I ask.

"Texas," Mom says. "They took off. Literally. In exchange for an easy divorce, your father gave up any right to see you. So all we get are his pitiful checks." By the time she pulls into the parking lot, she is winding down. "I know the humiliation of being dragged into a story you don't want. I won't go through it again. Do you hear me?"

I think I should save my breath, so all I say is, "Yes."

In suite 16-A on the second floor, Mom fills out papers. The carpet and walls are all a soft blue-green. I bet there are baby clothes that color.

They call me right away. The nurse asks if Mom wants to come but she shakes her head. "Just tell me the results," she says.

I follow this woman in blue scrubs and a cloud-print smock down a long hall. She opens the door to a darkened room and motions me in. There's a curtain to change behind. This time I get a cloth gown.

When I'm ready there's another woman in the room wearing a white coat. "I'm Rhonda," she says. "I'll be doing your ultrasound. Just step up here." She pats the table. "Stretch out. This won't hurt."

Once I'm in position Rhonda parts the blue-flowered gown, picks up a plastic bottle, and squirts warm jelly on my stomach. Rounder now. I can tell. Then she looks at the computer screen, types something, lifts a wand from somewhere, and begins to move it around where the jelly is. It doesn't hurt but it makes me remember the pain I felt there.

"Just relax," she says. I take a deep breath. "Good." She keeps the wand traveling. "Ahh," she says, then stops and types.

"Can you see her?" I ask.

"Please?"

"My baby. Can you see her?"

"The doctor in charge will read the results," Rhonda says. "He'll talk to you."

"Can I see?"

She turns the monitor and I raise my head. There's something bright in the dark background.

"Yes!" I say. "There she is!"

Rhonda shrugs her shoulders. "You can get dressed now," she tells me, lifting the lid on a little box by her side. "Here's a warm washcloth to clean yourself with. When you're done, go back to the waiting room. Someone will call you when the doctor's ready."

"Well?" Mom says impatiently, as I sit down beside her.

I won't tell, I think. I won't give this away. But my mouth says, "I saw her!"

"The doctor?" Mom closes the folder in her lap. She's been working.

"No," I tell her. "They'll call us when he reads the results."

"I hope they hurry," she says, and goes back to her file. They don't.

Mom works. I look through *Family Circle* magazines.

Too many recipes. Not enough babies. I guess I *will* have to learn to cook, but why are there no pictures of girls my age with babies? Don't we make a family, a circle? "Of course we do," I tell my baby.

"What?" Mom says.

"Nothing." I didn't mean to speak out loud.

Finally the door by the receptionist's desk opens. The cloud woman leans out and says, "McCauley?" We get up. Mom brushes off the front of her black jacket.

This time we turn left halfway down the hall and left again into an office with a large dark-wood desk and two pull-up chairs facing it.

The man behind it gets up. He's tall, angly, blond, and freckled. He reaches his hand across the desk. "I'm Dr. Demato," he says. "Mrs. McCauley?" Mom nods. He turns his hand to me. "You must be Julie." I nod, too. "Please have a seat."

"I *am* pregnant," I say. Mom glares.

"You are indeed," he says. Joy lifts me up on a golden tide.

"When?"

"Almost nine weeks," Dr. Demato tells me.

"No," I say. "When is she due?"

"The fact is," Dr. Demato breaks in, "this is an ectopic pregnancy. Sometimes the fertilized egg implants in the fallopian tube—"

Mom turns her face away, disgusted.

"Instead of the uterus," he goes on.

"I know," I tell him.

"A fetus like this is not viable, and its growth can rupture the tube, so you will need surgery to remove it."

"Does state insurance cover that?" Mom asks.

Before the doctor can answer, I say, "It doesn't matter. She's not implanted, really. She's just waiting."

Dr. Demato looks at me quizzically. "Go on," he says.

"She had to be sure I was ready and she was welcome, that's all. She couldn't settle in because Mom didn't believe I was pregnant."

"That's not relevant," Mom snaps.

I look at her. "But now you have to because Dr. Brennan and Dr. Demato both say so. Once I see a baby doctor, the baby will know and settle in the right place to grow." I am happy to have this clear.

Dr. Demato looks at Mom, who scoots forward in the blue chair.

"She's just—oh, she likes attention," Mom tells him, soft, like she's confiding something. "She likes *drama*, you know. And girls in high school having babies, I guess it seems special. But you and I know"—she leans toward him—"what a disaster it really is."

He waits a beat, taking in Mom's words. Then he says to me, "Julie, the body doesn't work that way."

My breath stops.

"The egg can't wait, like a car stuck in traffic, and then move on. It has to start growing or die. So it implants. But this one is in the wrong place."

"No, she's not!" My voice is fierce. "She's my baby. She's where she belongs!"

"I'm afraid not," the doctor says.

"Just wait awhile," I say. "A few weeks. You'll see. She'll move."

Dr. Demato shakes his head. "We can't wait, Julie. If the fetus gets much larger, your fallopian tube will burst and you'll be in danger of bleeding to death."

I jump up. "You can't! You can't take my baby!"

I grab something from the desk and throw it at him. "She's mine!" I yell. "You can't take her! You won't!!" And I tear out the door. Down the hall, through the waiting room, then another hall, down stairs with glass windows, out the main doors, across the parking lot. Mine! Mine! My baby!!

Tires screech as I cross the road and head down a hill into the woods. A quiet place. Good for babies. I stop by a little creek. My side hurts. I'll just catch my breath. Somewhere there's a safe place for mamas and babies. You'd think home would be safe. Or the doctor's office. Doctors protect life, right? Well, not this one. He's ready to get inside and take what he wants, just like that. So I've got to do all the protecting. This is my baby, my new life inside. No one else's.

That's why I have to hide in this shed. Cold. But safe. I'll close my eyes and think about next winter, when I'll hold this baby in my arms, maybe rock her in the rocking chair by the fire at Reba's house. There now. Doesn't that feel good? All cozy, Mama and baby. We could almost go to sleep . . .

Till a light burns my eyes and hands pull me up. A man says, "Julie," and I come at him like a cat, knocking off his glasses, throwing myself against and past him, but there's someone else and this one catches me, so I claw and bite and kick. Then they try to drag me. I curl up, curl up and lock, so no matter where they take me, they won't get her. I will hold her with my whole self.

nine

ZOE IS THE SWEETEST BABY. Nobody in the hospital thought I could carry her to term, but I did. And it went by so fast! Infancy is even faster. She can't crawl or roll over yet, but she gets a workout just kicking her legs and moving her arms like some jerky conductor. And she loves to study things. Give her a green plastic fish to hold and, if she's full and dry, you can watch a few minutes of bliss.

Zoe's a good sleeper, too. I put her down around ten and she's out till six-thirty or seven.

My biggest wish right now is that I could stay home with her, but with all our expenses, there's no way. I knew that when I had her. But I didn't know it would be so hard. Not the work, but handing Zoe over to Mrs. Jamieson every morning five days a week. This is not how nature intended mamas and babies to be.

At least Toyota has apartments for workers. Mom didn't like it when I moved here, but this way I have a little more time with Zoe in the mornings. She can sleep later and doesn't have to go out in the weather.

"How's it going, Jules?" That's Randy Crummond, getting off his shift as I come on.

"Fine. How about you?"

"Okay. Did you sleep well?"

"Great. Zoe went down a little early and—"

He shakes his head.

"She'd been so funny in the bath. She—"

"Jules! Look at me. Who am I?"

I just brush past him. "I've got to get to work," I say. "I can't let junk pile up around the line."

So what if he believes I'm unfriendly? I think, walking to the check-in station. The sooner I clock in, the sooner I'll be through, and I can take my baby and go home. Well, to our apartment. It's more like a motel room, to tell the truth. But it's fine for us. Perfect, in fact. No cooking and cleaning up. I can eat in the cafeteria, which means more time for Zoe. We have each other. That's all we need.

ten

I WILL NEVER LET ANYTHING BAD happen to Zoe. No one will hurt or scare her; she'll never be hungry, afraid, or alone. Not while I'm alive. I sat in that day care one whole day watching everything Mrs. Jamieson did before I agreed to leave Zoe there. I know what she's fed, how often she's changed, what they do at nap time. I know Allie and Mary Jane and Glenda, who also work there, and they know I'm paying attention. There's a lot in this world that would gobble little girls up. Dark places in every neighborhood. Most parents don't see, but I see. That's my job.

It's harder than this one, where I relay messages and keep the line clear. At work I know what to expect. My obligations appear and I fulfill them over and over. Then my shift is finished and I can forget about it. Not with Zoe. That shift is never over. I have to think, think, think: What does she need? How can I protect her? How do I choose the road that doesn't lead to disaster?

Mom won't talk about it. You'd think she'd be the

biggest help—the one person who'd really understand what I'm talking about—but she's been in denial ever since I refused to have an abortion. It's not just that she won't talk about Zoe. She pretends Zoe doesn't exist. Can you believe that? Her only grandchild! I guess it's some kind of mid-life crisis.

Then there's Reba, who promised to stand by me: she's not any better. I don't see her much anyway, what with work and Zoe. And the truth is, even if we're the same age and have been best friends since before we knew what best friends were, we're in different worlds now. She's still thinking about tests and papers and David Alton (who never thinks about her), and I'm thinking about Zoe and laundry and work.

She has come out here a few times in the evening, but she won't even hold Zoe. Says I should think about other things. What other things? I ask her. What else matters?

"Your life, Jules," she says, all self-righteous. "What comes next."

"What comes next is Zoe learns to turn over," I tell her.

"Jules!" Reba is exasperated. "I mean for you."

"That *is* for me," I tell her. "My next step: it's Zoe's."

Tears streak Reba's cheeks and glisten on her long eyelashes. She reaches out like she might take my hand, but I pull back.

"You're just jealous," I say, "because I don't have much time for you now."

Reba covers her eyes with her hand and her blond hair falls over her face. I feel bad for hurting her feelings, so I say, "Look, I'm not trying to be mean. When you have a kid of your own, you'll understand. When we can be moms together—"

But Reba doesn't want to understand. She walks out. Just. Like. That.

eleven

SOMETIMES WE HAVE GET-ACQUAINTED meetings at Toyota. People work together better if they know each other, and some of us live here so we have to get along in that way, too.

I don't take Zoe because of the germs. The one time I did take her Mike poked the blanket and said, "Is she a live birth? Is she? Is she? Let me see."

I backed away from him.

"If she's got problems, you know, death or devil, I can help." I walked out and took Zoe to the nursery. Meetings are no place for babies.

There's a guy named Vince who is always slamming his fist into his palm and saying, "Just show me the bastards who put me here. Just let me at them!" And Dr. Stapleton— he's an efficiency expert—reminds him that he came here of his own accord. Nobody made him take this job. This doesn't faze Vince. He's a small guy, not much taller than Damon, but muscular, like a boxer. His brown hair is cut close but shaggy like tree bark, and his eyes are ice blue.

He would be good to look at except his face is always clinched.

Then there's Hilda, who has curly red hair and dresses like a dancer: black tights, black leotard, paisley skirt, silver chain with a cross. Hilda looks too frail to work in a factory. Probably she works at the very end of the line putting in floor mats. She always asks the same things: "Why do we have so much weather? Who's in charge?"

"Weather just happens," Dr. Stapleton assures her. And Hilda looks around the room at us like she could say something rude but she doesn't.

"I have to be prepared," she says. "People could die from this much weather."

At which point Mike, who's tall and thin with clipped gray hair and a mustache, says, "We'll all of us die, ballerina. But I'm the only one who can bring people back to life."

Always the same joke and it's not even funny.

When it's my turn I try not to talk much about Zoe. I know people get bored hearing about babies. But there's no need to tell him about tending the line, and what else is in my world? Zoe and the line, that's it.

Oh, and memory.

So one day I tell them I have a dad but I never hear from him.

"Is he real?" Hilda asks.

I have to laugh at this.

"He's real and he's a pilot," I tell her, "so he knows all about weather. And he loves to cook. Or that's what I remember. Was always laughing."

My throat hurts when I say this, remembering the house when Dad was in it—he never lived in the apartment—feeling for a minute all that light.

"Is there more, Jules?" Dr. Stapleton asks.

"He would fix supper for us sometimes. Scrambled eggs with bacon and toast broken up in it. He called it Barnyard Dinner."

"Throw *up!*" says Hilda. Dr. Stapleton looks at her.

"It was great," I say. "Mostly because of the fun he had cooking it." This surprises me. I didn't even know I remembered it.

"How long since you've seen your dad?" Dr. Stapleton asks.

I have to think. Reba and I were in kindergarten when he left, so I would have been five.

"Years," I say. "More than ten."

"A long time to miss someone," he tells me. "Especially when they just disappeared."

"If he's dead I can resurrect him," Mike says. "Don't you worry, baby girl. Even if he's putrid in a ditch somewhere, I can pop him right back good as new."

This gives me an all-over shiver, and I'm grateful when

Dr. Stapleton says that's enough community building for the day.

What I loved about Dad was the way he whistled, the way he ruffled my hair. The way he made any room all right just by bouncing his happy nature around it.

I think about this when I'm back at work after community meeting. Dr. Stapleton reminded us that we all have jobs besides the one on the line, and he sent me to dust and clean glass in the lobby. People visit here, you know. They're curious about how cars are made. My Girl Scout troop came. Funny to remember that. I never dreamed I'd work here!

It comes over me while I'm straightening the magazines that the thing I loved about Dad—his joy—is exactly what Mom couldn't take. I remember coming into the kitchen once when Dad was whistling and making coffee and Mom was frantically looking for something in the drawer where she kept the bills. I didn't understand their conversation then, but the feeling scared me.

"How can you act so happy," she said, "when you know the mess we're in?"

"Well, I *am* happy."

"Do you know how infuriating that is?" she asked.

"I can see you're not pleased, if that's what you mean," Dad answered.

"It's like this all the time. You get above it all on your little airplane jaunts and leave me down here dealing with the consequences."

"I do all I can, Lana," he told her, his voice tired.

"No," she said. "You do all you *will*."

After Dad left I used to stand in their room, so full of his absence that it felt ten times bigger than it was, and try to smell the aftershave he'd used, the orange peel he liked to eat when the juicy part was all gone.

Dad only took one suitcase, so Mom had to clear out the rest of his stuff. What she didn't pitch, she boxed up. When I saw her toss his green leather paperweight into a black plastic bag, I couldn't stop myself. I cried out, "Mommy, don't throw that away!"

And Mom looked at me, her face blazing, then turning to stone.

"He threw us away, didn't he?"

I shut up. Selling the house and moving to an apartment meant throwing out a lot of things, but I kept a music box, a fairy tale book, and my baby blanket. I didn't know I was saving them for Zoe.

Mom thought my love for that blanket was dumb, but Dad thought it was funny. He thought *I* was funny.

A nuisance, too. "But you're *my* nuisance," he'd say, tying on my knit hat before we went out in the snow . . . or getting me more orange juice . . . or sharing his popcorn when I sneaked out of bed to watch a movie with him. If it got scary he'd reach across the couch and put his big hand over my eyes when the bad part came.

I thought he'd always be here to do that. Had no idea he'd trade me for an easy divorce.

Okay, this isn't good. Crying at work. Suck it up, Jules. Close it down. Can't have tears rusting the works.

I used to envy kids in vans like the ones we make here. That's a real family, I'd think. They have something that holds them all together and the van makes it visible. I felt that.

Stop. You've got Zoe. She's your family now. Get a grip on yourself.

This makes me laugh. Grip: like door handles—get it? And all the energy that would have flowed into tears sparkles out in laughter. I double over, hooting. One of the monitors calls me out on break.

She walks with me back to my apartment. I want to pick Zoe up early but she says, "No. You need this time on your own." We stop at the reception desk. Another monitor is working there. She unlocks the vitamin drawer and hands the pill in a paper cup to my escort. They wear white uniforms, too—so formal. It's probably the Japanese influence.

We stop at the fountain and the monitor fills the paper cup. Some sort of argument is going on in the little room with the TV. A big guy is picking up his chair and slamming it down. My guess is the line finally got to him. It's like he's still at work, banging those van doors into place.

This makes me laugh again. I'll have to tell Zoe I laughed myself out of work. I can tell her about Dad, too. Her *grandpa*. I never thought about that. He's hers, too. Dad and Zoe connect through me. Sweet.

twelve

I'M BACK IN MY ROOM NOW. After the crying and the laughing, the monitor made me promise to rest awhile.

If I had any money—my pay goes directly for room, board, and day care, so I never see it—I would buy some posters for this room like the ones my English teacher, Ms. Williams, had: a meadow, a forest, a poem. The walls are the color of old Silly Putty, chipped and gouged to boot. I'd get Zoe a mobile, too. Babies need bright things to look at.

Someday, Jules. Someday you'll be on your own.

Like Dad.

NO. Not like Dad. Not running away. Not abandoning. I'm running *to* a life with Zoe. I *want* family, that's the difference. Mom acts like it's good to be alone. She says that way no one can let you down. But I'd connect with relatives if I knew how.

Even Dad? Come on, Jules. Would you go to Texas looking for your dad?

Well yes, out of curiosity, even Dad.

I turn over on my stomach and my breasts hurt. Almost feeding time. With my nose up against the pink-checked bedspread I realize I don't even have my own smells here. The spread has a fabric-softener-over-disinfectant smell: fake lilac over fake pine. Lord. This is what I'm contemplating when I fall asleep.

I must wake up later, go get Zoe, have supper, and do all my evening things, but I don't remember. New-mother exhaustion. The next thing I'm really aware of is morning, when the door opens and a monitor barges in.

"Pack," she orders.

"Pack?"

"Yes, ma'am. You're leaving today, remember?"

"What about my job?"

"Now, they explained all this to you—"

I don't know what she's talking about, but I can tell she's not one for giving information. "Where are we going?" I ask.

"Wherever you came from," she says, her face all efficiency.

"That should be some trip," I say, but she doesn't crack a smile.

"I guess whoever brought you is coming to get you," she goes on, "so be quick."

By the time she gets to *quick*, I realize she means Mom, and I'm paralyzed. I can't do this. Management here is rude about Zoe, but they do have the nursery where every-body loves her. Nobody at Toyota would hurt a baby. I'm not so sure about Mom.

I want to crawl under the covers, to curl up in the closet in a ball. But something says, You can't. You've got Zoe. Moms don't crumple. Moms survey the disaster scene and figure out their options.

I look at my disaster: lost job, open suitcase, beautiful baby. I can't stay here. They just told me that. And I can't stay at Mom's. My whole life tells me that. But I'll have to be there long enough to figure something else out. I'll have to take care of Zoe and me in spite of Mom. How to do that I don't have a clue.

But I know how to put jeans and underwear in a suit-case. I know how to tuck the baby's clothes around them. How to gather up shampoo and toothbrush. How to change Zoe and see if she wants to nurse a little before our re-union with the grandmother who doesn't believe she exists.

Mom shows up. She has a meeting with one of the leaders—maybe to explain why I'm losing my job. Then she signs papers. She doesn't hug me. "Medication has plumped you up," she says, "but that will go away now that you're back to normal."

I want to say, What's normal about having to take care

of Zoe and hide her at the same time? but I don't. I have her under my coat, wrapped in my yellow baby blanket, secure in a sling I made from a long-sleeved shirt. I don't want Mom to start yelling and wake her.

The day is bright. Mom is all efficiency in her gray coat and black shoes. She turns the radio on as soon as the car is going. She isn't going to talk.

When Zoe grows up and has a baby I will be so proud of her! I will hold both of them close—my baby, her baby, the line of love that goes on forever. But Mom—she doesn't want to hold *me*, much less Zoe. "I'm not the touchy-feely type" is how she puts it.

I recognize the radio song. It's "So You." Damon sang it sometimes. "Gray is, the day is, but bright is my heart / knowing I'm part of your day, too."

Well, I'm not part of his day anymore, that's for sure. And how bright could Damon's heart be when he doesn't even want his own child? That's why I have to be so fierce, loving her. Loving her enough for her father and grandmother as well as her mother. Loving her like God.

Probably something you're not supposed to say.

Mom is talking.

". . . time for you to straighten up," is where I come in.

"What?"

"Stop the muttering."

We are in town now, driving down a street of old houses, huge trees.

"Just singing along," I tell her. Who knows, maybe I was.

"Juliet," she says, "I have put up with a lot. Can you imagine the talk I have to hear about your 'vacation' from reality? If anybody needs a vacation, it's me. Insurance only goes so far and, anyway, it ran out. You're not in danger and they won't keep you without insurance, so you've got to straighten up and fly right. See some counselor they pick for a few weeks—Lord knows what that will cost—"

"But Mom, I was *working*—"

She hits the steering wheel with the heel of her hand. "Stop it! You were not working! You were in the psych ward! And you had no more business being there than I do. The trouble with you is you don't know what trouble is. You've always been dramatic, but I didn't think even you would come up with a fake baby." Her voice goes on, chopping, chopping up her thoughts into words. I tune out. I know what's pushed her over the edge. She can't love Zoe so she says Zoe doesn't exist. And she has to defend her lie. We read about it in the psychology part of health class. That's why her voice is so loud, why she barely makes the corner turn from Windsor to Chandler. I'll call Reba. Reba was in that class.

And I'll be patient. For the time being I may have to take care of Mom and Zoe both.

Finally Mom turns left at the barbershop and pulls into the apartment parking lot. When we get out I try to wrest my suitcase from the backseat but lose my balance because of Zoe's weight in the front.

"Let me do it," Mom says, irritated. "It's that medication they have you on. But we'll wean you off of that. You won't need it now that you're home."

If Mom thinks I'm giving up the vitamins for nursing mothers that the Toyota doctor gave me, she's crazy. That's the one thing he was good for.

But I know better than to say anything. I haven't been her daughter for sixteen years for nothing. The way to deal with Mom is to keep quiet and do as you please but cover your tracks. I'm thinking this as I follow her up the metal staircase to our apartment.

"Home!" she says as she opens the door and flips on the light. You always need lights on in these rooms, darkened by the overhang of the walkway to the apartments upstairs.

I go straight down the hall to my room.

"Give me your coat," Mom says, but I don't want her to see Zoe.

"I'll hang it up," I say, opening my door.

Facing the bed with its tiger-stripe spread, I slip my coat off and lift the sling over my head. Zoe is still asleep, her golden hair frizzed out like a halo.

No baby bed, of course. For now Zoe will have to sleep with me, just like at Toyota. I put pillows around her on the bed. No need to take her out of her little cloth cocoon. If I wake her and she cries . . .

"Jules?"

"Yes, Mom," I say, coming out into the hall.

"I've got to get to work. I'm sorry but I've already missed half a day. There's ham and pimiento cheese for lunch. Or soup. I figure you can stay home and rest through the weekend, and we'll get you started back in school on Monday."

School? Is she completely crazy? School doesn't have a nursery like Toyota.

Cool it, Jules. Don't say anything, remember? You'll figure something out. Whatever's best for Zoe. That's what mothers do.

"Ham and cheese sounds great, Mom. You go on. I'll be fine."

"Don't go anywhere," she orders. "And I've put a pill on the table. Last one. Take it after lunch."

"Okay."

She almost falls over my suitcase getting to the door. She didn't even take off her coat.

thirteen

SATURDAY MORNING AND I GET UP EARLY. I want to get Zoe fed and bathed—I couldn't bathe her last night with Mom there—and ready for playtime before Mom gets up. I can tell Mom I want to hang out in my room or don't feel well or something till I get Zoe down for her morning nap. I can play music to mask the chortling. Isn't that pathetic? Hiding your heart's delight? Well, worse things have happened.

My plan is working pretty well till Reba shows up around ten o'clock. I didn't call to tell her I'm home. Mom must have.

Mom is running the vacuum and, while I hate the sound, it seems to soothe Zoe. She has just drifted off when the doorbell rings. At least I assume it rings. I can't hear anything but the Hoover, and then Reba's in my doorway.

"Hi, Jules," she says, almost shy. She looks skinny is all I can think. Skinny and real clean.

"Shhh," I whisper. "I just got Zoe down."

"But I thought—" Reba's face does one of those U-turns of emotion, shocked-and-embarrassed to oh-that's-cool. I pretend I don't see.

"So what's up?" I ask.

"Not much," Reba says. "I heard you were home and thought I'd stop by."

"Thanks," I say.

"Your mom says you'll be back in school on Monday."

"Mom is nuts. I can't go to school. There's no nursery there like they had at Toyota."

Reba's face gets flushed. "Oh, Jules . . ." she starts out. Then it's like her glasses steam up or something. I can't look at her face, so I notice the hole in the knee of her washed-out jeans and her GO BULLDOGS shirt faded from red to dark pink. Hand-me-downs from her big sister, Hannah. Maybe Zoe will have a little sister to hand things down to. I should save whatever she outgrows, save everything.

Reba just keeps looking at me till I realize she doesn't know what happened.

"I lost my job," I tell her. "I don't know why. Factory work is stressful but I can do it. I even got good at it."

Tears are pouring down Reba's face. Just pouring. She always was a crier.

"It's not that bad," I tell her. "I'll find something else."

"Can we talk?" Reba asks.

"Sure."

She takes the desk chair and I sit on the bed beside one of the pillows I've nested Zoe in.

"Do you remember . . . when we promised . . ." she reaches for Kleenex on the desk and blows her nose. I smile. She's always made this baby-elephant trumpeting sound when she blows her nose. I've missed Reba. I've missed being a kid. That's over, though. No going back.

Reba goes on. "When we *swore* we would always tell each other the truth, no matter what?"

I nod. "More than once," I said. "First, when we were so little we had that clubhouse under your back porch, and then in your room the night Hannah climbed out the window."

"Yes!" She is grinning. "You *do* remember."

"Of course I remember. You said even if circumstances should require us to shelter grownups from what happened—those were your words—we will always be honest with each other because—"

"'You have to have someone you can count on,'" Reba finished.

"Right."

"You still believe that?" Reba asks.

"Sure." I look down at Zoe, brush the warm velvet of her cheek with my thumb. Somewhere there's a baby who'll be her best friend someday.

"Okay," Reba says, and takes a deep breath. She rubs

her palms on the thighs of her jeans. "I love you, Jules. You know that?"

I nod. This can't be good.

"You haven't been working at Toyota. You've been in Meadowview."

"Meadowview?" It's this place they send people who are on drugs or have generally flipped out. "Bad joke!"

Reba laughs a broken sort of laugh and then I get it.

"You mean this is what they're saying at school? Somehow it seems better to be crazy than pregnant?"

"Jules—"

"Did Mom start this? It sounds like something she would do. It's what she thinks, after all. *She* should be in Meadowview."

"I came to see you there. Don't you remember? Your mother brought me. She said—"

"And you *believed* her? I don't get it, Reba. If sharing the truth is so important, what about *my* truth? What about mine?"

I grab Zoe up. I am fierce all the way through. "*This* is my truth, this baby girl!" My voice is louder than I mean it to be and Zoe wails just as Mom appears in the door.

"Get out!" I yell at Reba, at Mom, clutching Zoe's warm weight against my chest. "Don't come back till you can love her, too!"

fourteen

REBA TAKES OFF, LEAVING ME to my mother's fury. Mom jerks Zoe out of my arms and I'm not telling what she does.

Suddenly I am big, way too big for the room. I push Mom down, scoop up the baby, and run. All I can think as I run out the door is Save Zoe! Save Zoe!

Cool air and reality hit me at once. No coat, no extra blanket for Zoe. So I head for the laundromat across the street. Who's going to know I don't have wash going? If Mom comes looking here, I'll ram her with a laundry cart and take off.

I sit in the back on a gray plastic chair near the change machine. My heart is crashing around rhythmically like some part of the line at Toyota. I have to look at Zoe and I'm afraid, afraid of what Mom did.

I pull back the yellow blanket. There's a blue knot starting on her forehead, just above her left eye. Pale, like the veins on my breasts. Oh no! No! She's never been hurt before. I've let her get hurt. That perfect new skin, that baby peace has been broken. A tiny crack of blood shows. When I see that, my insides clench, deep where Zoe grew, as if I could take her back, cushion and shield her again. I feel a sound begin to travel up my throat. I can't stay, can't let it out here. I start for the door, lifting a warm blue towel off someone's cart. The woman's back is to me as she pulls clothes out of the dryer. Heading outside, I wrap the towel around Zoe in her yellow blanket.

Now what?

The grocery, I guess. It's close. Lots of aisles. I could hide if Mom came in. It's hard to get found there when you *want* to.

Then I remember the bruise. It's swelling on the outside. I know that's good. But what's happening on the inside? Maybe I should take Zoe to a doctor. What if something's pushing in, a big globe of blood against her brain? She is not moving much. Maybe she's just asleep, but maybe she's in a coma or something.

I don't know! I'm so stupid! I shouldn't have a baby! I can't take care of anything. I can't be trusted.

Stop it! Stop, Jules. It's your mom who hurt Zoe. Anyway, this isn't about you. You've got to help your baby. You're all she's got.

But where can we go? It's Saturday. Dr. Brennan won't

be in. I could walk to his office if he was there . . . but wait! What about the little clinic next door to him? Don't they have Saturday hours? Didn't Mom take me there the morning when I fell out of Reba's tree house and cracked my ankle bone? I remember how mad she was, how she said, "Jules, honestly, can't you even climb a tree?"

Forget Mom, Jules. Walk. On your healed ankle, with your strong heart. Heart that pumped blood from you through Zoe, heart that opened to take the blood back. One step. Two. Open. Close. Faster. Hold Zoe. Not too tight. Don't smother her. Turn back the towel, the blanket. Put your cheek to her mouth. Feel the kiss of her breath. Yes, yes, it says. Go on.

And you do. And the clinic is closing. Noon. A woman in a beige jacket is locking the door. "So sorry," she says. "You'll have to go to the ER."

"But my baby, a bruise—"

"The doctor's left. I'm just the receptionist."

"Please, look"

". . . not a doctor . . ."

"You have to!"

"The ER—"

"Can't walk there . . ."

"I'm sorry."

"Look! You don't understand. It's Zoe. She could die!"

I grab the beige sleeve. We're at her car now. I pull back the blue towel and the yellow blanket. I make her see. And the woman's face changes. She looks at Zoe and at me. At me hard. She knows this is serious.

Then it hits me: she may think I did it. I could go to jail, locked away from Zoe.

"Get in," she says. I do.

Don't think jail. Think help.

I am crying in the front seat. I don't mean to. Little stairstep cries.

"Okay," she says. "It's okay."

She drives to the university med center. It's the closest ER, and it's where Zoe was born.

"Thank you," I say, in big breathy words as we pull into the parking lot. I can breathe. Somebody else knows this is urgent.

When we are parked she comes around to my side of the car, and I see the car is blue, blue like the towel but not like her coat which is still beige and her shoes which are brown and lace up and Zoe will have to have shoes before long, at least those soft-sole pull-on shoes like Ms. Williams's baby had

and we are inside

where I'm letting go because the beige jacket has an arm on my shoulder to steady me while I fill out papers, and I realize I've never written my baby's name, not on a form, so I write bigger than the space allows in my best capital letters:

ZOE McCAULEY

I don't know her age, though, because I didn't have a calendar at Toyota, which I explain and which is okay, and they ask my mother's name and phone number, which I give them, because I have to and because I have help for Zoe now, and then we wait. I worry about all the germs in those rows of sick people. I keep Zoe wrapped up tight.

Finally they call my name, the rescuer says goodbye, and they lead me down a little hall to a room where I sit in a chair next to a desk across from an examining table with Zoe in my arms. A nurse stays with me. More waiting.

Finally a doctor appears.

"I'm Dr. Douglas," she says. "May I have a look at your baby?"

"Please."

Very gently she lifts Zoe from my arms and lays her on the examining table. I leap up, afraid. "Don't let her fall!"

"Don't worry. I'll take good care," the doctor says. And she looks and feels and strokes and examines and says there is nothing to worry about.

My knees almost go out from under me, I'm so relieved. I sit down to get my balance back.

"Everything's okay," the doctor repeats, wrapping Zoe up again, placing her back in my arms. "But I wonder if I might talk with you a little, until your mother gets here."

I freeze.

"If you feel your child has suffered an injury, it's traumatic for you, too."

"Sure," I say, swallowing tears.

"So we can talk?"

I nod.

And she looks at me through sparkling glasses with steady gray-gold eyes and she says:

"Tell me about your baby."

fifteen

THE JOY HER WORDS BRING IS SO HUGE I feel like my throat will break.

"Just breathe," she says. "Deep breaths." And I do, but there are some sobs and hiccups, too. "It's okay," she says. "Relax and your breath will come to you."

Slowly I begin to breathe evenly and Zoe's story spills out like jewels. Every wonderful horrible crazy beautiful part of it.

Dr. Douglas listens hard to let this happen. I can feel that. And I am so grateful that when I come to the end of my story I look right at her.

"Thank you," she says.

Don't make me leave, I'm thinking, begging the Universe. Don't take this away. I really look at her: tall, small-boned, with dark blond hair put up in a twist. Maybe if I keep this focus—

There's a knock at the door and a nurse hands Dr. Douglas a folder. Zoe's records. This makes me happy. It is written that she is real, that she needs well-baby checkups and shots. I can get these for her even without Toyota.

Dr. Douglas looks through the folder. Her face doesn't change. When she's finished she says, "Your mother will be here to get you soon, but I'd like for us to keep talking. Would it be okay with you if I arrange that?"

"Please," I say. "*Please.*"

"Good. And Jules, here's my card if you want to talk in the meantime. Don't hesitate to call anytime, okay?"

I nod. Can she mean this?

"You take Zoe and wait in the reception area and I'll work things out with your mother."

I'm shaking with relief and disbelief and don't have the energy or nerve to say, Lots of luck with Mom! "We'll come back," I promise Zoe as I kiss her forehead. "One way or another we'll come back."

When she walks into the clinic Mom looks like a storm on legs. She doesn't acknowledge us, just goes up to the window and pulls her wallet out of her purse. The receptionist takes her credit card and insurance card, then tells Mom Dr. Douglas wants to talk with her. Irritation and impatience cause Mom to roll her shoulders, stand straighter. She doesn't have time for this. She wouldn't have time on a weekday because of work and she doesn't have time on Saturday either.

"Weekends aren't vacation," she always says. "They're

for doing all the work and errands that piled up during the week. Free time? Huh! Not for a single parent. Your dad took all the free time when he flew the coop."

I can almost smell Mom's anger as she goes through the door Zoe and I just came out of. When she returns, her mouth is tight.

"Let's go," she says, and we do. "Are you hungry?" she asks once we're in the car.

I take a minute to locate my body, then find my stomach, feel the emptiness. "Yes."

"You want to go to the food coop?" she asks.

"That would be great," I say. "I could look at their baby soap and baby lotion, too." I am done with hiding Zoe.

She brings her hand to her forehead. "You mean you'll take that—that bundle in with us?"

"Mom, you can't leave a baby in the car!"

She lets out her breath in measured huffs. Her mouth opens but if there were words, she lets them evaporate. We've turned onto Danztler and passed the Shriners temple before she says, "Decide what you want to eat. I'll run in and get it to go."

A half hour later we are back in the apartment kitchen, sharing a turkey-avocado sandwich and spooning cups of tomato-basil soup. No sound but chewing and laying spoons on the table.

Finally I say, "I'm not hiding Zoe anymore."

"Evidently," she says.

"And I can't go to school till I find some day care." My hands are shaking but my voice is steady. Zoe makes me brave.

Mom looks at me. Surely her eyes aren't blurry. Suddenly she stands up, her lunch only half eaten. "You can stay home this week," she says. "That woman wants to see you again on Friday. Then we'll figure from there."

Relief hits me like the first pulse of a hot shower. I can't believe it.

"Thank you," I say. Thank Dr. Douglas, I add in my head.

"I'll have to work this out with Meadowview," Mom goes on. "They've got you scheduled to see someone else. I'll have to check insurance, too." She stands and sighs. "I've got errands to run—refilling your prescription, for one. That woman says . . ." She shrugs her shoulders. "You clean this up, okay?"

"Sure, Mom."

"And Jules, maybe you should take a nap."

That's a surprise. "Maybe I will," I tell her. "While Zoe is napping. Sometimes I did that at Toyota on weekends."

"Have mercy," Mom says, and leaves the room. Strange words for Mom. I have no idea what she means.

sixteen

SUNDAY I DO WHATEVER MOM SAYS, which is not much. We're just in the apartment in each other's way. Reba doesn't call, which makes me glad and sad. Zoe is calm.

Monday is easier, with Mom at work. Whenever I feel panicky, I remember I'll see Dr. Douglas soon. "Just a few days," I whisper to Zoe. And I figure out a routine for getting through the time. I sleep in—or pretend to sleep in—till Mom goes to work. Then I bathe Zoe, wash out her clothes, and hang them over the shower rod to dry. She only has four outfits, which barely gets you through the day with a baby. Soon I'll have to go to the thrift store. I don't want to shop there. It's okay for me, but for Zoe I'd like everything to be new—like her.

After bath and laundry I put her on a blanket on the couch, put on music and do baby gym, stretching and bending her arms and legs, pulling her to a sit-up position. Sometimes I dance with her in my arms. This makes us laugh. She nurses then and usually goes back to sleep. This is the hard time for me. I don't know what to do.

I would read but the baby books I have are about being *pregnant*, not about taking care of a baby. This all happened so fast that I hadn't gotten those yet. So I try TV, flipping through the channels to see if there's a show about babies, but I hardly ever find anything.

Then lunch.

Then Do Something Nice for Mom. This is important. Every day I pick out a task—clean out a cupboard, get the crud off the toaster oven, polish the teakettle—something to make her life brighter. She hasn't noticed yet but maybe she will. If Zoe is awake, I tell her, "I'm doing this for Grandma." Mom is Grandma whether she likes it or not.

I would like to take a walk after lunch but Mom's order still stands: "Do not leave this apartment." I reminded her that I'm going to need more diapers soon. "Don't worry," she said. "If you *really* need something, I'll get it." Come on! There's no debate about diapers!

But I don't want to rile Mom. She's letting me stay home and that's a lot. I know she hates it. She wants her life to be very organized, no surprises. But a baby rearranges everything. Your old life? Forget it! Mom won't get that back till we move out. I can't wait.

In the meantime, the afternoons drag. I play with Zoe. Sometimes I tell her about Dad. I hold her up to look out my window. You can't see much but the rooftops of stores, but there are some trees, and there's always the sky. I nurse and change her. And I tell her stories I can remember from kids' books I had: *Goodnight Moon* and *One Fish Two Fish Red Fish Blue Fish*. I can't remember the exact words, though, so the magic kind of leaks out. I wanted to save some of those books when we moved to this apartment, but all I could bring was the fairy tale one and Zoe's too little for that.

After stories, it's the TV again. Sometimes there's a baby on a soap opera or a talk show or even a program about medicine. We *do* have cable, thank God. Mom says it's her one extravagance. She loves the Discovery channel. I think that's weird. I mean, they *do* have good stuff and all. It's just that Mom seems so, well, anti-discovery.

Right before Mom comes home from work I put Zoe down for another nap. That's late, I know, but it means she's out of sight, at least for a little while, so Mom can settle down and I can help get dinner started.

After we eat I clean up the kitchen. When I'm done, I sometimes bring Zoe out into the living room and put her on the couch between Mom and me. Mom watches specials on things like giant sea worms in parts of the ocean no one has ever seen before.

She acts like Zoe is a bomb about to go off. She never looks at or touches her. If I talk to my baby, Mom jumps up and goes to the kitchen or the bathroom. When she comes back she sits a little farther away. This is sad but it's not my problem. There's nothing I can do about it. Just get through the days, Jules. Like waiting for a baby to be born.

seventeen

WHEN THE DAYS FINALLY PASS and I get to see Dr. Douglas again, the sun is shining. We are meeting at her office, not the ER. It's in a different building, closer to where I live. I can walk there, and it's a great day to get out with Zoe.

Dr. Douglas's office has mocha-colored leather chairs and a window looking out into a courtyard. It's a long room. We sit at the end where you come in. The other, bigger part, has her desk and an open area with large pillows in the corner.

"How has your week been?" she asks.

"Zoe is adjusting to being at Mom's," I tell her. "At first she didn't sleep well, but that's better now."

"And you?"

"If Zoe's okay, I'm okay," I tell her.

"I see," she says. "Last week you were in a crisis about the baby, so we didn't really get acquainted. I'm Emma. Tell me a little about yourself, Julie."

I don't like this. It feels smothery. I shake my head. "It's Jules," I tell her. "And I want to talk about Zoe."

"Okay," she says. "Tell me about her father."

"Damon? He was a kid."

"You, too," she points out.

"Not like Damon."

"How?"

"Sex for him was like a package of cookies we were sharing."

"And for you?"

"I wanted to be close to someone," I say. "I thought that's how I could do it."

"But that's not what happened?"

"No. His mother freaked out when he told her about Zoe. She sent him away."

"And your mother?"

"She didn't believe I was pregnant."

"So what did you do?"

"I went to the doctor by myself."

"And what happened?" Emma asks.

"He said I couldn't have the baby—she was stuck in the tube—but he didn't understand. I *had* to." My words feel hot.

"Why?"

"Zoe is mine. I couldn't let her go. I have to protect her."

"To keep her safe?"

"Yes."

SAFE is such a huge word.

"It's good to be safe," she says. "Everybody has that right."

I keep Zoe safe, but safe doesn't apply to me. I say this.

Emma tells me lots of people feel safe and never think a thing about it. This is like learning that some people smell music or hear color: impossible. But Emma says no, you can build safety for yourself, step by step. "Baby steps," she says.

She doesn't ask why I don't feel safe.

"If you are bad, you're not supposed to feel safe," I tell her.

"You're not bad," she says.

"You don't know me."

"I know that much," she insists.

Emma looks at me. She has her hair pulled back today and is wearing dangly silver earrings. In an oversize green sweater and black stirrup pants, she looks like an aging teenager.

I sit there. I feel a truth arriving, feel my bones get heavier.

Keeping Zoe safe makes me feel safe. I don't say this. Emma doesn't say it. But it is what we are talking about.

We're sitting in the same leather chairs, in the same

beige room where we started. No new air coming in. But something shifts as I sit here knowing this new thing: Zoe makes me safe. I feel my heart aligned with Emma's heart, like planets. I feel a huge sunshine in my chest because we know this, because my heart is with hers.

And I can't speak. Emma is quiet, too, but it's an active quiet. She is doing something. She is concentrating the energy that signals my heart. She holds me in this light.

After a little bit Emma asks about my family, about school. It's easier to talk now. When I get to the part about Dad leaving, my voice gets husky and my throat hurts. "Tears are good," Emma says. "Just let them come." I shake my head. Mom hates tears. They aren't worth it.

Emma doesn't seem mad when I don't cry. It's like it's up to me. "How do you feel about your dad now?" she asks.

"Like I made him up," I tell her.

"Hmmm," is all she says.

"Life when he was here seems so far away it's hardly real. Mom says I think he was better than he was, that it's not fair because he got to be the *fun* parent."

"Did he seem that way to you?"

"Kids don't know anything," I tell her.

She raises her eyebrows.

"I mean, who can trust what a kid says?"

"That's a very important question, Jules. It would be a

great place for us to begin next time. Our hour is up for today. Is this a good place to stop?"

"Sure," I say, though what I feel is No! No! I don't want to leave. Whatever she gave me—the connection with her heart—starts draining away with her words.

On the way out I get up my courage and blurt out, "Mom says I've got to go back to school on Monday. But I can't! I can't take Zoe and there's no place to leave her."

Emma puts her hand on my shoulder. "I'll talk to your mom and see what we can work out."

"Thank you," I say, for her touch as well as her words.

eighteen

EMMA MUST HAVE CALLED MOM at work because when Mom gets home she is stony-faced.

"That woman says to give you another week," she declares, setting four plastic bags of groceries on the counter without even shutting the door. "And she wants to see you twice. I hate to think what you are telling her."

I ignore that last remark. "Twice in one week?"

"Yes," Mom says, catching her breath. "Even when you're back in school she wants to see you."

I am thrilled. "Is there more to get?" I ask.

"There certainly is." I start for the door but she says, "You stay right where you are." Like I'd try to escape without Zoe.

Mom brushes past me, disappearing into the light. I walk in the kitchen to start putting things away. Cold things first, she insists, so I look for those: ground beef, milk, yogurt. Lettuce, green beans, broccoli. I've just moved to canned goods when Mom reappears. She picks up the conversation—well, her monologue—right where she left off.

"Add another week to surgery and Meadowview and this charade of you at home, and you will have missed five weeks, Jules, *five weeks* of school: almost a whole grading period! How are you going to make that up?" She is shoving cans and boxes into cupboards.

"Reba can get my assignments for me," I suggest. "I could start working now. It gets boring around here when Zoe's napping anyway."

"Oh, Jules," she says, whirling around so her full skirt, which she hardly ever wears, twirls. "When are you going to stop this?"

"Stop what?"

"You know what I'm talking about." She stands square in front of me, hands on her hips.

I just look at her.

"That!" she says, pointing toward my room.

"Her *name* is Zoe!"

"Z as in crazy," Mom spits back.

"Sick," I say. "You are sick," and walk out of the room.

I lie on my bed and try to think of another way, another place to be. This is not healthy. I can't run off to Dad in Texas, not that he would want us. I've saved a little money from scooping ice cream, but not enough to run away. What about staying with Reba? Her mom would keep us, I'm sure. But even Mrs. Karim can't go against Mom.

And there's no telling what Mom would do if I tried to move over there. She already acts like I've disgraced the family by having Zoe and then moving with her to Toyota so I could work. And then—I know. I lost that job, which embarrasses her. But it was the first full-time one I had, so I've got a lot to learn. No crime there. And as for being an unmarried kid with a baby, it's not like this is news. It happens all the time. For that matter, what about Mary? As in Jesus's mom. She had a really good story but I don't see how she got anyone to believe it. At least I had Damon. Not that Mom ever asked who the father was. "Zoe," I say, turning over on my side, "your grandma is really mixed up!"

At supper that night—omelets, which Mom can flip in the pan, her one cooking trick—I bring up schoolwork again.

"The best thing," I say, "would be for you to call my counselor—"

Mom barges in, "I've already talked to her once today. Don't ruin my dinner."

"Not Dr. Douglas. Ms. Adams, my school counselor."

"Oh, I talked to her a long time ago," Mom says, "right

after the surgery. She called to *inform* me"—Mom leans on the word to show how offended she is—"that you told her you were pregnant."

"Oh, yeah," I say. "I forgot I was supposed to have you confirm with her that you knew. Sorry, Mom."

"Not as sorry as I am."

How do *you* know? I want to ask, but instead I say, "The omelet's delicious."

We chew. Which sounds like "we choose." Okay, I'm going to choose. I choose to go back to my original topic.

"If you would call Ms. Adams Monday morning, she could get assignments from all my teachers. That might be quicker than asking Reba." Mom says nothing. I start again. "Or I could call Ms. Adams," I offer.

"You'll do no such thing," Mom says. "I'll handle it."

I bite my tongue to keep from asking Mom what she'll tell her. Anything but the truth.

"So you'll call her?"

Mom nods.

"Meanwhile I'll call Reba to see what I can get started on."

All weekend I try Reba's house but nobody answers. Sunday night she calls me back and explains that they went to her grandmother's in Paducah, which is as far west as you can go and still be in Kentucky. When I ask about home-work, she says, "You're coming back to school?" her voice all excited.

"Mom says I have to," I tell her. "But not for another week. She'll call Ms. Adams tomorrow to get assignments. I just want something to start on."

"Well, we're on Chapter 26 in French."

"*Vingt-six*? You're kidding."

"Glad to hear your brain's still working," she says.

"Yeah," I say. "But it's hard to think about school when it means leaving your baby. Besides, I don't have anywhere *to* leave her."

Still no Reba-words. Finally she says, "You'll figure it out."

"I hope so."

"It'll be great having you back."

"Thanks, Reba."

"And in history—"

"Whoa!" I say. "French is enough. Don't tell me any-thing else. I don't know where I stopped in that class but I think it was a long way back."

"Mr. Greene says we've got to *'Étudiez férocement'* to get where we need to be by the end of the year."

"He always says *'Étudiez férocement,'*" I remind her. *"Mais ne vous inquiétez pas."*

She laughs. "Hard not to be *inquiet* while studying *férocement.*"

"Maybe it's Zen," I say, thinking, Maybe it's a good idea.

"Speaking of homework," Reba says, "I'd better hang up and do some." We say good night.

"Ne vous inquiétez pas," I tell Zoe when I'm back in my room. Then I remember: you use a different form when you speak to someone you love. You call them *tu* instead of *vous* and so the verb form changes, too. It's one way people know when a relationship gets closer.

"Ne t'inquiètes pas," I say to Zoe again, kissing her on the cheek. "You are as close as it gets."

nineteen

SO I SPEND THE NEXT MONDAY and Tuesday trying to do homework anytime Zoe doesn't need me. First it's just French, since that's all I have. It's hard to do homework with a baby, even when she's napping. There's the problem of concentrating, getting my attention under control, and then when I do, there's a jolt of panic when I realize for an instant I've forgotten her. That's terrible! I don't want to study if it means forgetting Zoe.

But if you had a babysitter, I think, if you knew somebody else was focusing on her, wouldn't it be okay? But how can you *know* they're focusing on her? How can you trust someone enough to hand over your baby? It was different at Toyota. The nursery was part of the job. If anything had happened, I could have gotten to Zoe in minutes.

I like French. Reba and I have taken it together every year, though this year we're not in the same class. It's my second favorite class after English. If I can't concentrate on this, how will I catch up in history? chemistry? precalculus? I don't know how I ever did it all.

That girl was someone else, I figure. Having a baby changes you. My life isn't mine anymore. No, that's not it, because in a way it feels like it wasn't mine until I *had* Zoe. Maybe I mean it's not just mine. It's mine and Zoe's. Everything matters more, that's for sure.

Well, not French. Not *le plus-que-parfait et le passé composé*. They seem ridiculous. But graduating from high school seems a lot more important than it did. It's my ticket to providing for Zoe and having our own home.

Monday I get through half a chapter and Tuesday I write the assigned composition. It's supposed to be about some aspect of your family, so I have fun looking up baby words. At first I think what I need for Zoe is *le jardin d'enfants*, a day nursery, but then I realize that just means preschool and kindergarten. I need *des jouets*, some toys, and *plus vêtements de bébé* (more baby clothes). Not to mention diapers. Don't worry about that now, Jules. Just keep writing.

Tuesday afternoon I go see Dr. Douglas, who reminds me to call her Emma. She makes a bed for Zoe in the green armchair using throw pillows and a bed pillow so she won't scoot off. Zoe's not rolling over yet, but it could happen any day.

"How have you been?" Emma asks.

Now that I'm here it's hard to talk. I look at her brown suede boots, her chocolate skirt, then the caramel-colored tunic she's wearing, the brown and red wooden beads, and finally her face, relaxed but energetic, her gold-gray eyes resting on me.

"Trying to do French homework and take care of Zoe is hard," I say.

"Has she been fussy?"

"No. It's more a feeling in me. *I'm* fussy. I'm worried if I let my mind focus on French, if I forget for even a second that I have a baby, something terrible will happen to her."

"Many first-time mothers feel that way," Emma says. "It's a lot of responsibility to get used to."

I feel my shoulders relax as she says this. "So I'm not doing anything wrong?"

"Of course not! It will get easier. You'll see."

"Maybe. The first time I tried studying I got so worried that I wanted to put the book in the garbage and curl up with Zoe and take a nap. I wanted to get as close as could be so she'd know I'd never forget her. From then on, I made sure she was touching me as I worked, even though that meant sometimes I accidentally woke her up."

"You know she's safe here," Emma points out, "though you're not touching her."

"Sure. She's with me and I'm with you."

Emma smiles, pushes her hair back from her eyes. It's loose today and comes down just past her shoulders, like Reba's but not as bright.

"Good," she says. "I'd like you to try something then." She stands up and takes a quilt off a low shelf behind her. She spreads the quilt out on the carpet beyond where we sit. As she's doing this I see there are toys on the shelf, too. My heart glows thinking one day Zoe can sit on the quilt and play while we talk. I'm startled when Emma says, "Just lie down here on your side like you lie when you curl around Zoe."

"But I—"

"Just try it, Jules."

I feel awkward and strange but I do as she says, turning on my left side away from Emma, as if I'm between Zoe and the edge of the bed at home. But Zoe isn't there. She's over on the chair and it feels all wrong. I'm just about to say I can't do this when something weird happens. I feel myself getting small and cold. Nobody's with me and I'm afraid. I'm high up and about to fall. Breath catches in my throat and a small cry comes out, almost a toy cry, and then I feel Emma's arm across me, the shelter of her body on the floor nearby, and I start to cry so hard and loud I can't believe it's me. This goes on a long time. Emma must be kneeling. I feel her knees in the small of my back. But it's like she's holding me, too, and though I know I'm not supposed to cry, though Mom has told me and told me tears are weak, nobody wants a girl who cries, I can't help it. I keep crying till I'm nothing but hiccups, like a baby.

Like Zoe does sometimes. Emma sets a box of Kleenex in front of me, and I reach for some as I sit up.

Emma stands and offers me her hand. "Are you all right, Jules?"

I nod, take her hand and get to my feet, then blow my nose. "But I'm not supposed to cry," I tell her. "Mom says—"

"I'm sure your mom means well," Emma says. "But we all have to let feelings flow. Otherwise they make us sick."

"I can't get sick, I'm a mom," I say as I sit back down across from her.

"So whatever you feel, let it out," she counsels. "It's safe to do it here."

"Okay," I say, feeling like I'd cry some more if I hadn't run out of tears.

"Good. Between now and Friday, when you come back, I want you to ask yourself if there are places in your life where the feeling got stopped. Are there places it would be good to revisit?"

"No!" I blurt out. Then I'm afraid I've been rude. What if all at once Emma doesn't like me? Then what? "I mean I'll think about it, but it's not really good to look back. You just have to move forward."

"Is that something you've been told?"

"Sure. But don't you think it's true?"

"I believe it's not good to dwell on the past but that sometimes things happen that we close off, leaving part of ourselves stuck there. And it makes life hard not having all of ourselves in the present."

"I wouldn't want that to happen to Zoe," I say.

"Of course not. And the best way to prevent it is to check for stuck places in yourself."

"I'll try then," I say, still not sure what she's talking about.

"That's all I ask," Emma says. Then she looks at the clock. "I see our time is up. Is this a good place to stop?"

As Zoe and I walk home the wind is blustery, and I hold her tight against my chest. I feel sort of lit up and the sidewalk seems to push into the arches of my feet, giving me more energy with each step. "Zoe," I whisper, "the world is different than we thought. You don't have to be a baby to cry. And you can cry *hard*, a whole lot, and then get up and feel great!" I carry this knowing like a bright road within me all the way home.

When Mom arrives she has a list of assignments Ms. Adams faxed her. I take one look at it and some of the joy fades away. It's clear that if I *do* go back, I'll have to drop chemistry. There's no way I can catch up on the homework and the labs, along with French, English, humanities, and precalculus. I was barely making a C in chemistry anyway. I don't mention this to Mom, of course. Just thank her for the list and cross chemistry off in my mind. I'll deal with Mom if I have to. This is enough for now.

More than enough. I try to read a short story for English after supper, sitting in bed with Zoe tucked up beside me. But she gets fretful and nothing I do soothes her. Babies are very sensitive to what's going on with mamas, plus, who knows, maybe stress hormones come through the milk.

Whatever it is, she's not happy, so I pace with her in my tiny room, sit in my desk chair and hold her, swaying back and forth and singing:

Sweet little baby, my new one, my own
Warm in my arms, you are safe, you are home.

Mrs. Karim used to sing that to Posey, sitting in the blue rocker in the den.

Earth is your cradle, stars are your light,
Love is your blanket all through the night.

After a half hour or so of this, she drifts off to sleep. I'm sleepy, too, so I give up on homework for the night. I put

Zoe down, go out to the kitchen for a glass of orange juice, then sit with Mom on the couch. She's watching a show about giant insects of the tropics. We don't talk.

Later, when I get up to go to bed, she says, "I didn't know you could sing like that. It sounded good."

"Thanks, Mom," I say. Weird day, weird night.

Wednesday and Thursday are like that, too, with me trying to be in the school world, at least a little, yet not let go of Zoe. This wears me out. It's not just the assignments either. It's how my books smell, what I wrote in them, my old notebooks and folders. I thought the person they belonged to was over, but when I turn the pages again it's almost like that old self flies out. Like she's been looking for me. Maybe all that crying brought her back.

And I don't like it. I have enough to do to take care of Zoe and try to make up this stupid homework. I can't deal with the old Jules, too. Maybe I should just forget high school and get a GED.

I'm really glad when Friday rolls around and I get to go see Emma, even though I haven't done what she asked. I hope she won't be mad. How can I think about some trouble from the past when I've got all the trouble I can deal with right here?

twenty

AT BREAKFAST MOM ASKS WHY I SMELL like Vicks VapoRub. "Zoe's a little stuffed up," I explain, "so I put a tiny bit on her nose to help her breathe easier. Remember when you used to do that?" This seems like a friendly thing to say.

"God help us," is Mom's reply.

I go on eating my English muffin but I can't taste it anymore. After a while Mom asks, "You're seeing your *therapist* again today?" She makes the word sound ugly.

I nod. "At ten."

"Well, Jules," she says, standing up, "try to get this straightened out, okay?" She puts her dishes in the sink, brushes crumbs off the front of her black turtleneck. "I've seen about all this play I can take."

I know I should keep quiet but I can't. "Taking care of a baby and going to school is not exactly play."

Mom covers her eyes with her hand, then lowers her arm and straightens her shoulders. She's wearing her black-and-gray-checked pants with a thin belt cinched tight.

"I don't mean play as in *fun*," she says. "I mean play as in *acting*." On that word she lifts her hands over her head and shimmies them in the air. Then she pushes past me, grabs her purse and coat, and is gone.

She didn't brush her teeth. There's a whole lecture for that.

Walking to Emma's feels great. It's cool but the sky is blue and Zoe and I are like birds let out of the cage. If I make whispery sounds in her ear, she chortles.

Once in Emma's office she quiets down. I am lucky to have such a good baby. I've seen moms who couldn't have a conversation because of babies fussing and crying. Zoe's not like that. Mostly she either sleeps or looks around, sucking on her fingers. She's curious, taking it all in.

Emma wants to know how I've been. I tell her about the homework, how far behind I am, and how hard it is to concentrate. She says maybe some of this work could be deferred till summer, that maybe I could finish two classes now and two then.

"You mean go to summer school?" I ask. "Because I don't think I can. When I find child care, I've got to get a job."

"No," Emma says. "I mean getting an extension, an incomplete, so you can have more time to do the work. People do it all the time."

"Wow!" I say. "That would be such a relief." I can feel myself relaxing.

"I'll talk to your counselor—"

"Ms. Adams," I say, worried that Emma's next question will be about the homework *she* gave me.

Emma reaches for a clipboard on the shelf behind her and writes Ms. Adams's name down with a pen attached by a chain.

I don't like the chain. It reminds me of PE and roll call and races. Of recess and boys. Whistles, pushing, sweating. It makes me see locks and bigger chains, zippers, sand.

"Jules?" Emma's voice sounds far away. I see her in front of me, her long gray skirt. Black boots maybe. Something rose, too. A shawl? I try to focus on her but I have to close my eyes. Something is pushing at me. Pushing back, dragging me forward, I don't know. And I don't want to go. I want to stay here! I fight it. If I can keep my eyes on Emma's face . . . But the force shuts my eyes. It comes after me. I pull back and twist in the chair, twist to the right, trying to hide. He's got that chain around his neck and it swings close as he leans in, saying BAD! BAD! you good-for-nothing worse-than-shit nobody wants you no one will believe you IF YOU TELL it's your fault they'll send you away no one could love you look what you did   what you made me do   a nice boy   with your filthiness   I have to hurt you to make it better.

Maybe I say something. Emma's voice is far away, like

stars. She is putting a blanket over me. She is tucking it close. I feel her hands, small, around the edges of me. Like Zoe's hands.

"You're all right," she says. "You are having a memory. But this is not now. Now you are here with me. Safe. Just breathe." And I do.

It takes a while, but when I've settled down, she asks if I want to tell her about it.

"Not now," I say.

"What do you want?"

"Where's Zoe?"

"Look in your arms."

And there she is, looking up at me, her wide eyes steady like Emma's.

"If you can't talk about what happened, perhaps you could write about it at home."

I shake my head. "Nothing happened," I tell her. "I imagine things."

"It didn't look imagined."

"I'm good at it," I say.

Emma is quiet. Then she says, "Sometimes the body remembers what the mind can't bear to until a small thing, maybe a song or a smell or an object, opens that memory. Did anything like that happen just now?"

I see the chain again. I can't. I won't. "No," I tell her, my jaw clenched, my throat tight.

"Just let it settle then," Emma says. "We'll talk more about it next time. Is this a place where we can stop?"

I nod and stand to go. Emma rests her hand on my arm cradling Zoe and says, "Don't forget. I'm just as far away as the phone."

"Thank you."

"You've worked hard," she says.

My eyes sting but I don't say anything. I pick up my backpack, which I can only get over one shoulder without putting Zoe down. Emma holds out her arms. I hand her Zoe and feel tears start. No one has welcomed this baby but me. I swipe my face with the back of my hand, get myself together, and go.

The walk back to the apartment is delicious. The air seems fresher, the sky more blue than gray. When I come to the quick mart at Woodland I go in and get a Coke.

"How old is your baby?" the cashier asks, skinny, with a big gob of green gum in her mouth.

The question scares me because I'm still not sure. I'm so stupid, stupid. How can I take care of Zoe if I don't even know how old she is?

"A month," I say. She can't really see Zoe because I've got her wrapped up and held close.

"A shrimp," the cashier says.

Fear digs deeper. Is something wrong with Zoe? Emma didn't say that. Is she not growing right? What should I do? My heart is pounding and I feel light-headed.

The cashier's claw is holding out change.

"It's a girl," I say. "It's Zoe."

twenty-one

MY DELICIOUS DAY IS GONE. The cashier's words are a huge cloud blocking out the sun. Who can I ask to look at Zoe? Not Mom. Can I call Emma? She gave me her card and said any time.

Okay, okay, I tell myself, walking by the insurance building, the vet's, the grocery. Don't panic. Moms can't do that. They have to stay in control for the baby's sake.

Get home. Take a deep breath. Call Emma.

So that's what I do.

The receptionist takes a message and says Emma will call between appointments.

While I'm waiting I sit on the couch with Zoe on her blanket beside me. In her clown sleeper, half pastel blue, half pale yellow, she does her baby workout, bicycling her legs, punching the air and doing cheerleading moves with her arms. She gurgles and coos, sticks her tongue out, enjoys every bubble she blows.

But should she be rolling over? Sitting up? I grab the phone on the first ring.

"Jules, it's Emma."

"Thank you." Tears press my throat but I don't cry.

"What's going on?"

"I'm afraid Zoe's too little for her age which"—I can hardly say this—"I don't know exactly. I'm afraid something's wrong with her."

"Did something happen since you were here?" Emma asks.

I tell her about the cashier.

"Do you have reason to believe she's an expert on babies?"

"I don't know. I guess not."

"Did she really look at Zoe?"

"No."

"So don't give your power away," Emma advises. "Trust your instincts. Does Zoe seem okay to you?"

"She seems perfect," I say.

"Well, then, relax. If at some point you get worried again, call me."

Hanging up I can hardly believe how relieved I feel. "You're fine," I tell Zoe. "You're just right."

It occurs to me that since Emma has Zoe's records, I can find out her birthday. I want to know this! I want to know the most important day of my life. And I can ask the next time I see her. Asking is okay if you're safe.

What I am now is worn out, so Zoe and I spend the rest of the afternoon on the couch in front of the TV. Soap opera. Oprah. Soap Oprah. That's funny! But it's not very interesting. No babies.

Then Mom comes through the door with a big brown bag stapled shut. "I got Chinese," she explains. "To celebrate."

"Something at work?" I ask.

"No, Jules," she says, setting the bag on the counter, sliding her purse off onto the bar stool. She turns and smiles at me but it's a wavery smile, like it wants something. "To celebrate you. Getting back to your life."

This is really strange. I don't know what to say except "Thanks." Mom is not the celebrating type. But whatever she's carried in smells great, so I put throw pillows around Zoe and go in the kitchen to set the table. Mom lifts white cartons out of the sack and presto! Chicken and snow peas, ginger shrimp.

Halfway through the egg roll, when I've taken too big a dip of mustard and the inside of my nose feels like it's on fire, Mom asks, "How was your visit with Dr. Douglas?"

"Good," I say. "I was worried if Zoe's growing fast enough but she told me everything is okay."

"Jules—" Mom pauses, fork above her plate.

"What?" I say.

She glances toward the living room. "Did you hear something?"

I jump up and run in to find Zoe happily tasting her toes. "She's fine," I tell Mom as I come back to the table.

"Yes, well," Mom says. I hold my breath. Then she shrugs her shoulders and says, "The chicken is good, don't you think?"

"Delicious," I tell her, so relieved that the shadow has passed over and on.

That night when we're tucked into bed I think how great it would be to know someone who *was* an expert on babies, or who at least *had* one so we could talk. There were girls at school who had babies but not anybody I knew. They were pretty much shut out. How's that for cruel? You can be really cool, having sex with your jock boyfriend one day, but if you get pregnant, you're an outcast the next.

Oh, but my English teacher, Ms. Williams, was *married* and pregnant. That's a whole different story. All fall I watched her get rounder and more in her own world. Sometimes she'd be so involved in what she was teaching that she'd miss what else was going on. I remember one day around Halloween when we were studying this poem:

Some say the world will end in fire

I can see that poem in our literature book, printed over a mixed picture of flame and snowflakes.

Some say in ice.

The day Ms. Williams talked about it, a guy called Zappa who sat across from me spent the whole hour stabbing his compass into the page, not to draw circles, just to pock up the picture.

From what I've tasted of desire

Was it wanting something that got Zappa to destroy that page? Was the poet's name Frost? No, I must be making that up to go with ice.

From what I've tasted of desire
I hold with those who favor fire.
But if it had to perish twice,
I think I know enough of hate

Maybe it was hate, not desire.

I think I know enough of hate
To say that for destruction ice
Is also great
And would suffice.

Ms. Williams never noticed Zappa. She didn't see Steve Rentsler drop a water balloon out the window either. She was pregnant and she loved poems and she talked inside a bubble that day, a shiny poetry-pregnancy world, all hers.

I loved watching her. She was so complete in herself. There was every excuse for her. All she had to do was breathe and she was doing her job. Even if she wasn't the best teacher, even if she was a bad person (which she wasn't), a liar, nothing but filth (things she would never be), it would be okay because she was doing something good in spite of herself. Inside of herself. So much good was being done through her, she could make up for anything. A baby was becoming. A poet maybe. A father. A sister. Ms. Williams had offered herself as a door to the world and . . .

Something wakes me. It's Mom opening the door to check on me. I don't move. When it shuts, I try to will myself back to class, will myself to hear Ms. Williams talk about the poem. But Ms. Williams isn't there. It's a substitute, Mrs. Miller. And it's not Halloween anymore. It's almost Thanksgiving. She says Ms. Williams is in the hospital.

"I guess the baby's coming," somebody calls out.

"Let's hope not," Mrs. Miller says. "It's too soon."

twenty-two

THEY HELD THAT BABY OFF FOR A WEEK, which I didn't know they could do, by keeping Ms. Williams in bed and on drugs. I read about the drugs later in a book I got out of the library. After the birth, she had six weeks off, which meant Mrs. Miller stayed on as our teacher. But Ms. Williams brought the baby in to show us one day right before we got out for Christmas.

"Why's he all mashed like that?" Mike Gilespie asked.

Ms. Williams beamed. "He just hasn't unfolded yet is all," she said. "Babies are like roses. They're still buds when they're born."

"Blooming babies!" somebody said, and we all laughed. This baby business, plus having a teacher be so human, was making us nervous.

Ms. Williams was lovesick, you could tell it, which brought up a horrible possibility: what if our mothers had loved us like that? And then, almost worse, what if they hadn't?

Lying in bed, covers cocooned around me, I remember that day.

Her baby, Kevin. No, Connor. How she held him up for us to see but wouldn't let anybody get close because of germs. How he took up an enormous amount of room for someone who was the size of a small watermelon and could basically do nothing but be.

BE. Bay-BE. Mom-ME.

And of course Damon and I had already found each other by then. Underneath our clothes, I mean. In early October. And everybody knows by third grade that that can get you pregnant. But we were careful.

We took no chances. Except by breathing. Except by having sex.

It was after Ms. Williams brought her baby, it *was* after that, on the weekend, that I managed to roll the Trojan off right before Damon slid inside me. Guys play Russian roulette, daring death. I dared life. Just that once. I'd already put the foam in, so it didn't seem a big dare. And Damon was too far gone to protest. Afterward he did, though. None of that holding and singing, my favorite part. No. He was super-pissed.

"Are you crazy? Do you want to ruin the rest of your life?"

"Yes. Absolutely. I do."

"This is no joke, Jules," he said roughly. "I can't have a kid and travel with a band."

"Oh, calm down," I said. "I'm not getting pregnant after one time. Anyway, I used foam."

"Don't be stupid," he said. "There's a lot of people walking around who were planted in foam."

"How do you know?"

"Coach told us in health."

"Well, nobody told the girls."

And then we got to talking about how unbelievably lame it is that they separate us for sex ed, in some last-ditch effort to keep us from getting together.

I told him how Mrs. Carter showed us a video explaining periods even though we'd all known about periods since we were reading the *Little House* books.

And Damon said he was totally freaked out when Coach showed them a series of slides of a woman's vulva and vagina—her "parts," Coach called them. True, most were afflicted with warts or herpes or some other plague, but one was normal.

Damon went on, " 'That's not just real accurate,' Coach told us. 'Really it looks more like a strawberry.' Ralph started laughing then and pretty soon everyone was hysterical and Coach told us he couldn't believe what a bunch of kindergartners we were. Then the bell rang and we were leaving class, and I was still totally AMAZED at what I'd seen right there in Stuart Ellis High, and Ralph came up beside me and said, 'Could you believe that?' 'No,' I said, and was about to go on being amazed, when he said, 'That guy is still using a slide projector! We should have had a movie, man!' "

Curled up in bed like that baby suspended in the middle of the class, the middle of the poem, the middle of Ms. Williams, I can't help but laugh remembering this. Laugh to myself. And it is the most amazing thing. It scares me, all the air and light I breathe in after the laughter goes out. But it is sweet, too. Sweet as a baby laid against your chest. Sweet as the hope of morning.

But morning brings the memory that Mom said I'd have to go back to school next week. When I was with Emma I got so caught up in being there that I forgot to talk about what next. I could call her up, I think, but no, I've already done that. Don't wear out your welcome, Jules. Grow up. Figure something out for yourself. Besides, it's Saturday and you don't want to bother her on the weekend.

I feed and change Zoe but she's still drowsy, so I put her down in her pillow palace after I make the bed.

Mom is in the kitchen eating her weekend egg.

"Hi," I say, reaching into the fridge for OJ, the cabinet

for granola. "What are you up to today?" Maybe if I can get her to talk about herself she won't ask about me.

"Grocery store, oil change, bank statement," she says. "And cleaning up this dump."

This dump means she's depressed, so I say, "I'll do it."

"You'll do what?"

"Sweep, mop, dust." As long as you won't ask me anything, I think. As long as you don't mention school.

"Feel free," she says, and then, softer, "Thanks."

We're at the table now, her white plate and my white bowl on navy blue placemats. Juice glasses, Mom's coffee mug. There's nothing pretty on this table, I realize. I look around the room. I don't know what I'm looking *for* but it's not there. Nothing personal, nothing extra. It looks like nobody in particular lives here. Blank as the silence we sit in.

I'd better say something before she does. And before I think about it what pops out of my mouth is, "I think I'll take Zoe and go over to Reba's house today."

Mom looks up sharply. "You won't take that—" All my muscles tighten to help her stop that sentence. It works. "I'm sure she'll be glad to see you," Mom says, "but—"

"I'll clean stuff up here first," I tell her.

"Okay," she says. "Be back for dinner."

The one advantage of living in a shoebox is that it

doesn't take long to clean. Well, ours doesn't since Mom doesn't allow clutter. She is always getting rid of stuff.

While Zoe naps and I vacuum I think about what I told Mom. Can I really take her to Reba's? I haven't been there since I got pregnant. What if they all act like Reba does, too embarrassed or ashamed to admit I have a baby?

Mrs. Karim won't. She likes to remember. And she loves babies. She'll love Zoe and understand why my life is different now. Maybe even—this just hits me as I scoot the coffee table over to vacuum there—maybe if I went back to school, say just half a day, she would *keep* Zoe!

I could pay her *some*thing, somehow. When my job money is used up, maybe she'd let me clean for her. I could walk to Reba's house, leave Zoe, and then catch the bus with Reba. After morning classes, I'd walk back, pick Zoe up, and go home. Of course it's a long walk from school to Reba's house, but hey, I'll figure something out.

Relief makes me almost giddy. Now I have something to offer Mom. And part of me, much to my surprise, smiles at the idea of going back to school, even though the homework seems impossible. If Mrs. Karim looked after Zoe, I could enjoy it because I know Zoe would be safe and loved. I wouldn't have said I enjoyed school before, but right now getting away from Mom and this apartment sounds like a vacation.

As things are, I'd have to get a GED pretty soon anyway to support Zoe. I might as well actually graduate.

Imagining Mrs. Karim with Zoe makes me realize how much I've missed her, her house full of life. Hannah, Reba, Posey. Mr. Karim in his study on weekends working on cases or in the den watching football. Emma would like them. Feelings just flow there, events, too. They don't get choked up.

Zoe cries and I go in to change and play with her, then bring her out to the living room and put her on the couch while I dust. The long-sleeved shirt sling I brought her home in doesn't work if you bend over. I need one of those front carriers like Mrs. Karim had for Posey. I wonder if she's still got it. I could ask! I could even ask about the baby clothes.

That idea feels so good, as if in our dark apartment with its bare brown couch, end tables empty except for plain lamps, I am standing in a shower of sunshine. I can ask Mrs. Karim about Zoe! She can tell me if everything's developing on time and what I should do next. She can *help* me! Dust rag in hand, I laugh and cry at this. "Zoe," I say, picking her up and hugging her close, "things are going to get better. I've got another mother to talk to."

twenty-three

SO WHEN I'M DONE I CALL REBA.

"Jules!" she says, her voice full of surprise. "What's up?"

"I wondered if I could come over this afternoon and bring Zoe. I'd like your mom to meet her."

Silence.

"Are you busy?"

A long pause. Then, "Hold on. We were going to a movie, but let me check. Maybe we could do that tomorrow."

She lays down the phone. Please, please, I think. I need to come now so I can ask Mrs. K. and have a plan about school to tell Mom.

"Mom says great," Reba says. "Can you come for lunch?"

"Sure. I was just about to fix something."

"See you soon."

I put Zoe in her green sleeper with the white rabbit over her heart. She's wide awake, arching her back, hard to change. As I'm wrestling with her it hits me: she's trying to roll over! I am thrilled! I lift her high and dance around the room. She laughs, honest to God. Hiccups, too.

It's a quick walk to Reba's if you cut through Lily Park. I'm a bit nervous as I ring the doorbell. If I weren't I'd open the door and call out "It's Jules" and somebody would yell, "Come on back. We're in the kitchen!" or "Reba's in her room. Go on up."

Posey comes to the door. She's grown since I saw her, and her brown hair is short now, wavy.

"Hi, Jules," she says.

I want to hug her but I don't. "I brought my baby," I tell her.

"Reba said you would."

We just stand in the entryway with its bench and books, coat rack and backpacks.

"Where is she?" I ask.

"In the kitchen with Mom."

Still Posey doesn't move, so I shrug my coat off and hang it up, then step past her through the hall and into the yellow kitchen. Pots, pans, plants, glasses: everything winks light.

Mrs. Karim turns away from a big bowl of something she's mixing and wraps me and Zoe in a hug. "Welcome home!" she says.

I will not cry.

Reba has a stack of multicolored plates she's dealing out at the table. "Hey," she says. "Tuna salad."

"Great." I want to introduce Mrs. Karim to Zoe but I don't know how. Though I felt at home a few minutes ago, now I feel awkward, on the outside. Maybe I shouldn't have tried this.

"Let me take the baby," Mrs. Karim says. "You girls go on and eat while we get acquainted."

I put Zoe in her arms and say, without meaning to, "Mom has never held her."

Mrs. Karim looks straight into my eyes. "Maybe she thinks she's too young to be a grandmother," she says. Then, carrying Zoe, she leaves the room.

Reba sits down. "Should we wait for the others?" I ask.

"No," she says. "More for us." So I sit down, too. She passes a basket with pita bread, then a plate of sliced cucumbers and chopped tomatoes. "Oh, drinks," she says, jumping up. "Milk? Iced tea?"

"Milk would be great," I say. Milk is good for nursing moms.

The tuna salad tastes good but I can barely swallow it. Something is bothering me. "Your mother didn't look at Zoe," I tell Reba. "She just stared at me."

And Reba says back, fast as a slap, "That's because Zoe isn't real."

As if she'd punched me in the stomach, I double over

and throw up the one bit of sandwich I just ate. Reba jumps up, touches my shoulder, grabs a roll of paper towels, runs one bunch under the faucet, then hands it, dripping, to me.

"I'm sorry, Jules. Put this on your forehead." Then she squats down at my feet to clean up the pile of puke.

I get a vision of high school, the hall just outside Mrs. Feeback's door, Reba taking care of me.

"You did this at school when I was pregnant," I tell her.

"Were you?" she asks.

"What?"

"Were you pregnant?"

I'm over the gut-punch now. I stand up.

"This isn't good for me," I say.

"We've got soup," Reba offers.

"I don't mean the food. I mean your refusal to—"

"—to lie to you? I do refuse. I can't see how you'll ever get better like that."

I start toward the door, then turn around. "Better? You don't know anything! I am *worlds* better since I had Zoe! I've got my own life, somebody to care about. You can't imagine. You've always had *this*." I sweep my arm around to indicate the family, Mrs. Karim, the house, all the energy and motion that's in it. "Till I had Zoe I was living on the moon."

"Please don't go, Jules," Reba pleads. "Please sit down."

I hesitate. I'm furious at her but I also feel how much I've missed her, missed her whole family. Mrs. Karim has Zoe, I tell myself. Just relax. Hear Reba out. So I sit down.

"Of course I was pregnant," I tell her. "I went to the doctor."

"And what did he say?"

I don't like that question.

I could lie.

Reba and I don't lie to each other.

Anyway, he was wrong.

"He said it was an ectopic pregnancy." Reba had health class. I know she knows what that means.

"And?"

"And—oh never mind. It doesn't matter. He was wrong."

"Wrong or not, what did he say?"

I am tearing my pita bread into little chunks, then mashing the chunks with my fork. It doesn't mash well. It's pretty dry. I drizzle a little milk on it.

"Jules!" Reba's voice gives me a start. "What did he say?"

"He said there wouldn't be a baby."

"See?"

"See?" I leap up, mad as fire. "Do I see? What about you? You're the blind one. It doesn't matter what he said, what anybody says. They're wrong. I have Zoe!"

I push past Reba and run into Posey in the doorway. She looks scared.

"Where's your mother?"

Posey points toward the den, on the other side of the dining room.

When I get there Mrs. Karim is sitting in the blue rocker with Zoe. Except for Zoe herself, it's the sweetest thing I've ever seen.

"I have to go now," I tell her, reaching down for Zoe.

"Bless you both," Mrs. Karim says, holding her up.

I'm halfway past the dark dining room table when I remember why I came. I turn back.

"Mrs. Karim," I call from the doorway. "I wanted to ask you a favor."

"Go right ahead," she says. She is still sitting where I left her.

"Well, Mom wants me—and I need—to go back to school. If I do, would there be any way you could keep Zoe, just in the mornings?"

"Of course," she says, getting up and coming toward me. "Anytime you want. It would be great for you to go back—not just for you but for Reba, too. She's missed you, Topaz."

I laugh and Mrs. Karim pats my back. I'd forgotten the nickname she gave me: Jules = jewels = topaz. And that made Reba *Ruby*. Now I see *topaz* ends in z, which is where Zoe starts.

"Thank you, Mrs. Karim," I say. "That will be perfect."

I grab my coat from a peg in the hall. And despite Reba's crazy refusal, Zoe and I go waltzing home.

twenty-four

I DON'T TELL MOM THAT NIGHT. She doesn't mention school and I don't want to get her started, so I just chop onions and peppers for the stir-fry and listen to Mom talk about her work. It's not as if she likes it, but what else has she got to talk about? And today is Saturday!

"Last week this woman came in to apply for benefits. Terminal cancer. I tell her it takes up to six months to get approval and I ask if she's got that much time. This *offends* her. Good grief! I have to know. If she's going to die next month, I don't want to waste my time or that of every worker who has to process her papers."

"It *is* kind of a sensitive question," I venture.

Mom comes right back. "She should have thought of that before she came in!"

After that I don't comment. Eventually she asks if I went to Reba's. Nothing more.

That night I dream I'm back in Emma's office. I really want to be there, want to talk to her, but I can't keep my eyes open. The light pouring in the window is too bright and the arm of sleep is around my waist, dragging me under. I struggle to stay awake, to focus on what Emma is saying, but it sounds like a foreign language. The tiny part of me that isn't filled with sleep is sad and panicked. I'm wasting her time, Mom's money. And I need help.

In the middle of the night I wake up. The dream washes through me, makes me want to stay awake, but it's not possible. In a few minutes I plunge into the dream again.

This time I'm running and can't open my eyes. Running fast, around curves, maybe in our old neighborhood. This is crazy, I think. I could get killed. But I can't stop or even slow down. The sun is bright on my eyelids. They seem to be scarred shut.

When morning finally comes I am *not* rested.

I check Zoe. She's still asleep, so I take a shower. By the time I'm clean and dressed I feel better. The day is bright and sunny. I decide that after breakfast I will take Zoe to the park.

"You'll do no such thing," Mom says over our breakfast of toaster waffles.

"Why not? Didn't you take me to the park when I was little?"

"That's not the point," Mom says, stabbing a waffle corner.

"What is it then?"

"Don't tempt me," Mom says, getting up to pour more coffee. I see that her narrow black belt is twisted in the back.

"What's that supposed to mean?"

She turns to face me. "How hard can you make this?" she asks, putting her hands on the back of the chair.

"I'm not *making* anything," I say. "I just want to take Zoe to the park like other mothers."

"But you're *not*," she says, leaning forward, almost snarling the last word.

My stomach clamps down. "Not what?"

"Not like other mothers," she says, and walks out.

What is wrong with Mom? Is it my age? She knows girls my age have babies. She's a social worker. Besides, nobody at the park has to know I'm Zoe's mother. I could be her big sister or the babysitter.

I consider telling Mom this as I scrape the plates, rinse off the syrup, load the dishwasher. But it's useless. Mom only sees what she believes is real. That's the problem, isn't it?

Mom comes back down the hall as I'm heading out of the kitchen. "I've got to work on taxes," she says. "But first let's talk about school."

"Okay." Here goes. Zoe's taking a long nap. I've got time.

Mom walks into the living room and I follow. We sit on the couch. And I notice something.

"Where did this come from?" I ask, fingering the yarn on a green and gold afghan that's appeared on the back of the couch.

"My mother made it," she says.

"Where was it? I've never seen it before." I pull the afghan down to cover my lap.

"I have a suitcase of her things," Mom says. "Stuff I picked out when I went back to Illinois after she died."

"I don't remember that."

"I should hope not!" she says, almost a laugh in her voice. "I was barely pregnant with you."

"What happened to her?"

"Jules," Mom says, her let's-get-this-done voice back, "we need to talk about school."

But I *felt* something from Mom and I don't want to let it go. "I know," I say, "but just tell me what happened. She's my grandmother, after all." You know what? Zoe has made me brave. I would never have said that before.

In a quiet voice, Mom says, "I don't know exactly."

"You don't *know*? How can that be?"

"She was sick all my life with some chronic illness and finally it killed her," Mom blurts out.

"But what did the doctors say?"

"The *doctors* didn't say anything, Jules." Now she's mad. "There *were* no doctors. My parents—your grandparents—were Christian Scientists and prayer was supposed to be our medicine."

"You mean you let her *die*?" I know that was the wrong thing to say as soon as it's out of my mouth.

"They never listened to me, either one of them. Dad traveled all the time for work and I was left with Mom, who might get into a crisis—pain, diarrhea, not being able to eat—and me not able to call a doctor. There was my little brother, too—"

"You have a brother?" And I have an uncle? I think. Maybe cousins.

"Jules, this is *not* what we need to be discussing. We have to talk about school. You're set to start tomorrow?"

"I have a plan," I say. "But Mom, this is important. Tell me about your brother. I never knew I had an uncle."

"Well, basically you don't. He's not speaking to me."

"Why?"

"Because I'm not speaking to Dad, since he let Mom die, and Jeff sides with Dad."

"But what happened?" No answer. I try again. "If your mom was sick, who took care of you?"

"*I* did. Took care of Jeff, too. And I tried to take care of Mom. Even called an ambulance once when Dad was out of town. But—oh, Jules, I can't talk about this! The only good thing about it is it's over and done with." Mom has threaded her fingers into the weave of yarn and her hands are shaking. She takes her hands back. "Now for your plan."

I take a deep breath. "Well, Mrs. Karim says she'll keep Zoe in the mornings, so I'm thinking if you could drop me off, I could catch the bus with Reba, then leave at lunchtime and—"

"That's not a plan, Jules. That's a fantasy."

"Well, I can't leave Zoe here by herself and I can't ask Mrs. Karim to baby-sit all day."

"How could you bring Sara Karim into it?" Mom is spitting mad now.

So I get mad, too. "Because she *cares* about me!" I say, afraid all at once I will cry. Don't do it, Jules. Not here. "She cares about *Zoe*! Like a real grandmother," I finish.

Mom looks at me like I just slapped her. "You are going back to school tomorrow morning. I will take that, that *bundle* to work."

Everything in me rises up like a wave. "You will *not*!" I say. "You will not touch her!!!" I get up, pushing the afghan into her lap. In two breaths I'm down the hall and back in my room.

And Zoe is gone.

Panic starts like a siren, but then, like magic, a feeling of calm shuts it off. This is a game. I know it. I can play, too.

"Zoe, are you hiding from me?" I ask, almost purring. I peel back the blue towel, the yellow blanket. "You must have learned to roll over and fallen off the bed."

I'm on the floor now, lifting the bedspread, looking under. No Zoe. So I crawl around the bed, the chest, the desk, over to the closet. She's not on the floor. She must be *in* the closet. Clever baby, learning to crawl, opening that door. "Zoe," I sing, "Come out, come out, wherever you are!" and, still on my knees, I slide the closet door open. There she is! Sitting up with her fingers in her mouth! "Zoe, you bad baby!" I exclaim, scooping her into my arms. "Best baby," I whisper, nuzzling her hair.

I try to act calm for her sake, but I am scared. She's never done this before. I tell myself that's what life is: doing what you've never done before. That's how babies grow. But moms have to grow, too. And what if the babies grow faster? What if they *outgrow* their moms? Can that happen? Why don't I *know* anything? And why won't Mom help me?

Easy, Jules. Just hold Zoe and breathe. Hold on to Zoe. That's it. Baby steps. Kids run away from home. Even babies do, evidently. But you found her. You're a good mother. She's right here. But if she can crawl, she'll walk soon. Then what?

The rest of the day I carry Zoe around. She's squirmy,

but I'm afraid to put her down. I give up on homework, except a little reading for English. The assignment looks short, but that's because it's poetry, so forget short. I can't concentrate, just roll my eyes over the pages. And silently dare Mom to bother me. True to her intent, she spends the day at the kitchen table working on taxes. We have leftovers for dinner and don't mention school again.

I go to bed uneasy. What if Zoe disappears while I am asleep? I put the desk chair against the locked door so she can't get out. I think about belting her to me somehow, but I'm afraid I might roll over and hurt her because she can't get out of the way. After lying there forever, feeling like some live wall, I drift off. My last thought is I can call Emma tomorrow.

Pounding wakes me. Then Mom's voice. "Jules! It's seven o'clock. Let me in!"

I jump up, grabbing Zoe. Scoot the chair away from the door, turn the button lock, pull the door open.

"You should have been up half an hour ago!" she says. "You'll miss your bus and I'll have to drive you."

"I'm not going," I say. Mom is already showered and dressed, navy blue something, pale blue something. I do not care. "Go away," I tell her. "Leave us alone."

But she shoves herself into the room like some bad wind. "I told you I'll take"—there's a glitch in the voice— "*her.*"

She reaches for Zoe and I jerk away. "You think I'd hand her over to you? You hurt her! You gave her the only bruise she's ever had." And I look down, to make sure that the bruise has truly faded from Zoe's face. That's when I see she has done it again. Made off with herself.

"Mom! She's gone!"

Mom just looks at me, astonished.

"She can crawl now. She did this yesterday. I found her in the closet."

"Jules—" Mom's voice sounds very strange.

"Help me! We've got to find her!!" I check the floor, under the bed, the closet, then push past Mom and do the same search in her room.

"Calm down," I hear her saying. Calm down? She's crazy.

"My baby is missing!" I yell at her, checking the bathroom, pulling towels out of the linen closet. Mom's hand is on my shoulder.

"Jules," she says again. But I whirl around, push her out of the way, and fly through the living room, the coat closet, the kitchen. Oven. Cabinets. Under the sink. Where could she have got to? What if she's stuck? Hurt?

"We have to move the refrigerator," I say, putting my sweaty hands on it, throwing my weight into it. Useless.

"Jules, please!"

"Come on, Mom! She could die back there!"

"I promise you, she is not behind the refrigerator."

Mom's voice is so flat, so certain. That's when I know. "You took her! You did it!! You!!!"

She steps toward me. "Jules, I didn't touch her. I've been with you the whole time. She wasn't there."

"Yes you did! You hate her! You hate me." I'm screaming now. I raise my arms and start hitting Mom in the chest. She grabs my wrists.

"Stop it!" she says, pinning my arms. I kick her. She lets go of one wrist and slaps me across the face. "It's good news if you can't see her, Jules. It means you can rejoin the rest of the world."

Her words hit harder than her hand, and I make a sound I've never heard before. It hurts coming out of me. And it drags tears out with it, years of tears forbidden in her house.

Mom steers me over to the couch. Otherwise she doesn't touch me. When I finally stop crying she brings me a blanket and a cup of tea. How stupid does she think I am? There's something in there to make me sleep, then she can do what she wants.

She's on the phone. Probably calling work. Thinks she'll drop me at school and go in late. Huh! When she turns her back I'm calling the police.

But she doesn't turn her back. She comes over to the couch instead. "Dr. Douglas wants to see you," she tells me.

"Now there's a trick," I say.

"Not a trick," Mom answers. "I promise."

"But I have to find Zoe!"

"I told Dr. Douglas that. She says she can help."

I hate it. I hate leaving without Zoe. But I've looked. I've looked everywhere. Mom is handing me my coat.

"I can't find her!" I wail.

"We're going for help," she says.

I think of Emma with me when I cried. I hold on.

twenty-five

"IT'S OKAY, JULES," Emma says. "You are here. You're all right. Put your feet on the floor and feel yourself grounded in the earth. Take deep breaths. That's it. You are on solid ground. You are at home."

But I'm in a river, I want to say. I'm being pulled away from Zoe by fast muddy water. Still I can hear Emma's voice far away. And I think how people on the shore throw a lifeline and pull someone who's drowning out of the water but you have to grab the rope and so I open my mouth to reach back with my voice but all of a sudden I start to shrink. I get smaller and smaller, my body contracting, my spirit trying to hide. There's sharp pain in the back of my neck, something pressing into it.

"I'm very small," I say, my voice high.

"Where are you?"

"In Larry's room."

"Who's Larry?"

"The boy around the block."

"Is he small, too?" Emma asks.

"No. He's big."

"What is happening?"

"He says what a good girl I am. How pretty. He takes off my panties."

I say these words, but I am not there anymore. I'm out the window of his room through the screen like the breeze in the tree like a bird so high and small while he is doing what he's doing.

And the light is on my skin, light, even if my neck is jammed into the bed rail. Far away that bad little girl. He has to do this to make her better. That's what he says, only she's so bad it doesn't work. She knows that, doesn't she? Yes, she does. Even in the tree she knows that. Her mother told her about bad girls when she touched herself where he touched her. "Larry hurt me," Jules had said, scared to her bones. "He hurt me here."

"Stop that!" her mother commanded. "He's a good boy. He would never do such a thing!"

"But Larry—"

"You hear me? Nothing happened to you."

Jules knew she should shut up. She knew she should. But she was so lost that she had tried again. "He put his hand—"

And Lana's own hand had lifted and swung down and

smacked the fire out of her. "I don't ever want to hear this again! Your daddy's gone, didn't even take his mess, and you come home with this story!"

Jules had cowered by her bed. Her mother was right. It didn't happen. Bad was in her, like Larry said. Not out there.

Larry wanted to get the bad out of her. He would try hard. If she would just be quiet, not cry. Of course it hurt. Didn't she think it hurt him? It was supposed to hurt. When she cried or squirmed or if she ever said no, she put the bad back in. And if she told, they'd never believe her. All the bad would come back and she'd be nobody's little girl. Nobody would want her then.

Only Larry wanted her now, really wanted her. He said she had to come back to see if he'd finally got all the bad out. Then she could be his princess. And then she'd never have to take her clothes off. She wouldn't make him do these things anymore. He wouldn't have to hide like that and be afraid like she made him. Not many boys would do what he did for her. She was so lucky. He put up with her—all her filth—right there—it made him crazy, that dirt he could not get out. She saw how wild his eyes got and how there was spit around his plump lips when he threw his head back. She could see this even from the tree. See that little rag doll under him—if you go limp, it won't hurt so much—that little rag of a girl he wiped himself with.

She could see that girl now only bigger, shrunk into a ball in Emma's chair. And Emma was coming over to her, even to the tree, and taking her hands and saying, "This is a memory. You are here. It wasn't your fault. Something terrible was done to you."

And the warmth of Emma's hands pulls her back from the tree into her body again. It's okay. Here she's safe.

Emma holds my hands. Home is what it feels like. Like holding Zoe.

Then I remember. I jerk away. "Zoe's gone!" I say.

"No, she's not," Emma says. "Zoe's always with you. Stay here now, Jules. Stay with the little girl you were."

I shake my head. I want to tell Emma no, but I can't talk. I want to get away but I'm tied up.

"What's going on?" she asks.

I'm five years old, somewhere dark. I hear Emma but she's so far above me, like a bird, then farther, much farther, like the sun above the roof of the garage when I'm trapped, and I can't speak for what is forced in my mouth. I can't breathe. I am choking.

"Breathe," Emma says. "Put your feet on the floor. Breathe," she says again.

I try to do this.

"What is happening happened a long time ago. To the little girl that was you. Not to you now. You grew up and you are strong. You can go and get her."

Her words lift me up, and I do see I'm not only my small self. She is there, but *I'm* here with Emma's voice like a hand leading me through a dark place.

"You can go and get her," Emma says again. "Right now."

And then I'm in that garage with its smell of motors and concrete, tobacco and wet sand, and I see my plump legs in red shorts, my bare arms in the white sleeveless top with the rickrack heart on the front. My brown hair is coming loose from the ponytail. I am curled up, arm bent over my face to protect my head. Someone should come and get me. Where are they? Someone should put a stop to this. The big people should come.

I'm big now. I could carry her. But Emma says I've got the baby. I can't put her down.

"I can't!" I say to Emma, my voice breaking. "I've got Zoe!"

"Jules," Emma says. "Stay here. Stay with this little girl."

"I can't—"

"Do you want to leave her there?"

Her anklets are muddy like her blue tennis shoes. He is gagging her now.

"No!" I cry. I bend over and wrap my arms around her and pick her up. Without putting the baby down. Without losing. "Zoe!" I croon, rocking back and forth with the trembling child in my arms.

"Something big has happened," Emma says when it's over. I know, I know. "You've traveled a long road." I nod. But all I can think is, Don't send me home. I belong here.

"Would you like to go home and rest?"

I shake my head.

"Jules—"

"I want to stay with you."

"You have me here," she says, touching her heart.

I look at her like I understand, but I don't think her words work. I want this room, her voice. Nowhere else. No Mom. No lost.

"Our time is up and I have to stop now," Emma goes on. "But if you need a little more time, you can rest in the room next door while I talk to your mom."

"Please," I say, and she shows me down the hall to a tiny room with a daybed. I lie down and Emma covers me with an afghan from somewhere. This feels very sweet.

When she leaves I cry myself out and start to fall asleep.

But panic jerks me awake. Where is Zoe? I get up, fold the afghan, and go out in the hall, first walking right, which leads not to the lobby but the stairwell and a door. What if I went out wherever that door leads? What if I walked away from Mom forever?

I stand there imagining. Where would I go? How? I don't even have my backpack. No jacket. No money. No Zoe!

I retrace my steps and find Mom in the hall outside Emma's office.

twenty-six

GOING THROUGH THE LOBBY is like watching a movie.

We walk to the car, drive to the apartment, everything different. I am solid. But there's something I don't understand, an emptiness trying to catch up with me.

When we get to the parking lot I bolt out the door, run up the metal stairs, forgetting I don't have my key.

Mom comes up behind me, unlocks the door. I streak to my room. How can I have left Zoe this long?

Someone took her, I tell myself. But she'll be back now. Yes. She'll be napping.

The room is empty, like it never had a baby in it, just a bed with a pile of pathetic pillows and a yellow blanket nested in a blue towel. Inside the blanket, there are socks knotted together. Five of my white socks, one with something stuffed inside. To make a head. I must have done this. I can't breathe.

Then I go to the chest, jerk open a drawer, and rummage through underwear, jeans, and T-shirts. No baby clothes.

I'm sweaty and my heart is pounding. I know. I know. I have known. This is why Reba can't see her, why Mom won't. Zoe!

Whatever holds me up lets go and I fold down to the floor. A moan comes out of me. I wrap my arms around my knees, trying to hold myself, to shield myself from this truth arriving. But it's too late. I rock and cry.

Zoe isn't a baby I had. Zoe is me.

How can this be?

And why didn't Emma tell me? She had to know all along. She tricked me! She pretended to see Zoe so I would trust her. What a fake! She took what I gave her and led me on—

I want to scream, but all that comes out is this low, low sound, like a hurt dog.

If I don't have Zoe, what have I got? No future. Nothing. I throw the knot of socks across the room.

I am crouched against the wall now in the narrow space between the corner and the chest. Nowhere to go. If I stay here long enough, I'll feel nothing, I tell myself. Like a rock. But no, I'm more like a seed.

Then all of a sudden I see myself from up in the corner of the room and I know what I am: a grown girl crouched like a baby. I am someone waiting to be born.

I look up and Mom is standing in the door.

———◦❙❘❙◦———

I get up. I am so empty, like wind chimes walking. Mom comes forward, and when I meet her she lets me rest against her chest and puts her arm around my back. I don't make a sound.

Mom is warm. I'm shaking. She asks if I want tea. No. A bath? That sounds good. She fills the tub as if I were a little kid. You were her baby, Jules. She bathed you like you bathed—no, don't think about that.

When she's gone I slip out of my clothes and into deep warm water. I see my breasts and belly—with a red line that must be the surgery scar—my pubic hair. No baby came out of this body or nursed from these breasts. This is the same body Damon panted over, the same one Larry—

No, that was a child's body, a little girl's. That was sick.

A long time ago. A long, long time. You'll never be caught there again. You went back and got that little girl, remember? She's here with you in the bath. That's what Emma says. That little girl, not Zoe. Except she is Zoe, too. I have to take care of her, so we're having our bath.

I don't see how I can do this.

Look, Jules: you took care of an invisible baby, why not an invisible little girl?

Very funny.

I'm not trying to be funny. I'm sleepy.

Sleep then.

I wake up in cold water and put in more hot. Can you live in the bath? It feels so good, like rocking. I fall asleep again.

I dream of a woman drumming. She's standing, playing a big drum with her hands. The rhythm is wonderful. It makes my heartbeat stronger.

I wake up. The water is still warm but I'm ready to get out.

twenty-seven

BACK IN MY ROOM I HUNT for clean clothes. How did all my stuff get in such a mess? Jeans wadded up in the drawer, shirts piled in the bottom of the closet. Clean? Dirty? What have I been doing?

Baby laundry, Jules. Make-believe baby laundry.

Never mind, never mind. I pull on a wrinkled pair of jeans, find a yellow shirt I never wear on a hanger. I'll have to sort through all this stuff. Yeah, I think, this and a lot more besides.

But not now. What now? At first I have no idea. Then it comes to me: I want to talk to Reba. Not on the phone. I want to go over there.

Mom is in the kitchen working on taxes.

"Why aren't you at work?" I ask.

"I thought we could both use a day off," she says. "We could talk."

"I want to go over to Reba's."

Mom looks at her watch. "It's late and you haven't eaten anything. How about some lunch?"

"I'm not hungry."

"A snack then." Before I protest, Mom pops bread in the toaster, takes hummus out of the fridge, moves the tax piles to the counter, and deals out silverware and plates.

I see I have to do this. I fill water glasses while she slices a tomato.

Once we're at the table, it's like my vision focuses all at once and I see she doesn't look so good. She's lost weight. The green blouse she's wearing is too big and the wrong color. There's no light in her eyes, and she looks more than her usual tired and aggravated self. She looks, well, lost.

"Jules," she begins, a quaver in her voice.

I look at my plate. Don't say anything, Mom, I think. Please, don't. But she goes on.

"Dr. Douglas talked to me about . . ." Mom hesitates, smoothes the turned-up edge of her placemat. "About what happened to you."

I want to run.

"I'm sorry," she says. "Jules?" She reaches across the table, puts her hand on my arm just above the wrist.

I nod, forcing myself to stay in the chair.

"I'm so sorry."

"Okay," I say. "Okay, Mom. Thanks."

"It must have been when your dad was leaving. I . . ." Mom sounds like she's going to cry. Not allowed! She knows that. It's her rule. "Well, that's no excuse," she says.

I don't answer. What could I say? She is opening the door on a room full of bones. I try to eat but it's like the food is from another planet. Who could swallow this stuff? I stand up, light-headed. Like always, I clear the table, load the dishwasher, but I feel so strange, stretched out, a line from the earth to the sky. As I turn to leave, Mom puts both her hands on my shoulders.

"Don't stay late," she says.

"I won't."

"And call when you start home."

"Mom!"

"Please," she says.

That's a first. "All right, I will." I take off.

On the walk over I'm thinking, What if they're not even home? What if they're taking Posey to dance class or something? Well, I'll figure that out when I get there.

I walk past the pizza place—mmm, smells good. Past the shop where people spend big money on running shoes, past the children's bookstore in the yellow house. I could have gotten books for Zoe there. No, Jules, no, you could not.

That's why Mom didn't want me to take her to the park.

Oh, shit. I see now. People would have laughed. Somebody could have turned me in. That woman who took me to Emma at the ER, *she* saw . . . Stop it, Jules. One thing at a time. Baby steps. You be the baby. You take the steps. This time you're going to see Reba.

I cut through Lily Park with its huge trees, baseball field, tennis courts. I avoid the playground, do not think about the baby swings. I walk by the pool, the bandstand. My heart hurts, thinking about bringing Zoe here. I feel that future torn away from me, a future that's in the past now. I don't know how this can be. My chest is so heavy. I want someone to hold me. Someone strong, steady, who was here before, who is here after. But there are only strangers in the park. And trees. So I go up to a huge tree, an oak maybe, and lay my hand on it. The funniest thing, when I do that it's like my heart lifts and opens. I put my face against the bark, my arms around the solid body of the tree. Tears come. I hold on and this is good.

I feel steadier when that's done. I have a friend now, a friend past Zoe. I don't care if it is a tree. I look carefully to memorize exactly where my tree is—the third from the bandstand, the fourth from the path toward the skateboard ramps. I'll come back, I tell my tree. Thank you.

I don't say this out loud. I don't want to look crazy. Am I crazy? Was I crazy?

Jules! Baby steps.

I don't look at any babies in strollers. I get to the Renfro Avenue edge of the park and head on up to Reba's house.

Mrs. Karim's car is in the driveway. This is good. The front door isn't closed all the way but still I knock.

"Coming!" Reba yells.

She bounds down the stairs wearing purple sweatpants and a bright blue T-shirt.

"You're dressed like an Easter egg," I tell her.

"Jules!"

We look at each other.

"You don't have . . ." she ventures.

"No," I say. "You were right."

And now it's Reba who bursts into tears. I barely get her in a hug when she starts jumping up and down and saying, "Jules! Jules! This is so great! Thank God!!! Mom! Mom!" she hollers. "Jules is here. She's back!!!"

And Mrs. Karim appears in the entryway. She sees I'm empty-handed. "Oh, baby," she says, and takes me in her arms.

"Thank you," I say. She gives me a deep hug, then lets go. "Thank you for pretending Zoe was real," I tell her, then turn to Reba. "And thank you for saying she wasn't."

"What happened?" Reba asks.

"Can we sit down first?"

"You two go on in the den," Mrs. Karim says. "I'll bring you something to eat. You look starved, Jules."

I just ate, so I'm not starved but I look like a refugee for sure—my clothes rumpled, my hair long and tangled.

In the den, Reba and I sit on the old brown leather couch. We used to pretend its arms were horses and we'd ride the range, then have a make-believe campfire and sleep out under the stars. It was all so real. Like Zoe.

"So tell me," Reba says.

"How long have you got?" I ask.

"The rest of my life," she answers.

And I realize, sitting there, looking at my best friend from forever, I've got the rest of my life, too. Somewhere past all that's missing is what I've got. Emma will help me find it. And Mom—I don't have to think about her now. Right now I'm safe here with Reba, who wants to know what happened.

"It's not pretty," I start. "But it's the truth."

"That's what matters," she says.